MALORIE BLACKMAN

A.N.T.I.D.O.T.E

CORGI BOOKS

A.N.T.I.D.O.T.E.
A CORGI BOOK : 0 552 52839 0

First published in Great Britain by Doubleday,
a division of Transworld Publishers

PRINTING HISTORY
Doubleday edition published 1996
Corgi edition published 1997

7 9 10 8 6

Set in 11/14pt Monotype Plantin by
Phoenix Typesetting, Ilkley, West Yorkshire.

Corgi Books are published by Transworld Publishers,
61–63 Uxbridge Road, London W5 5SA,
a division of The Random House Group Ltd,
in Australia by Random House Australia (Pty) Ltd,
20 Alfred Street, Milsons Point, Sydney, NSW 2061, Australia,
in New Zealand by Random House New Zealand Ltd,
18 Poland Road, Glenfield, Auckland 10, New Zealand
and in South Africa by Random House (Pty) Ltd,
Endulini, 5a Jubilee Road, Parktown 2193, South Africa.

Printed and bound in Great Britain by
Cox & Wyman Ltd, Reading, Berkshire.

For Neil and Elizabeth
with love

Contents

Prologue

I'm in deep, deep trouble. And like the biggest fool in the universe, I'm about to wade out even deeper still. But I don't have any choice.

Because they've got my mum.

I've been warned that I'll never see her again if I try anything – anything at all. I know they're watching me so I'm having to think fast. All I've managed to come up with so far is this. It's not perfect, it's not ideal – it's not even clever, really – but it's all I can think of.

I'm going to record the whole story on Mum's computer – then back it up onto disks and give them to Nosh with a message saying, 'If anything should happen to me . . .'

When people do that in films, I always think 'Yeah, right!'. It's such a cliché!

If anything should happen to me . . .

In the films they always know that something is going to happen to them. Why else would they leave those kinds of instructions? But in my case, I really don't know what's going to happen. I wish I did. Even if it's going to be something . . . bad,

I wish I knew.

Not knowing is the worst thing in the world. With everything that's happened, I daren't even hope. I can appreciate now how Marie Antoinette felt in her prison cell, waiting to have her head lopped off.

I don't have much time. It's very hard to try and sort out my thoughts, but I must. It's difficult when all I keep thinking is that if certain people have their way, in a few hours' time, Mum and I will 'disappear' – never to be seen again. So I'd better get this right. I'll make sure that if Mum and I do 'disappear', then those responsible don't get away with it. I'll tell everything as best I can – just as it happened.

Everything.

It's Wednesday now. Late afternoon. Ten past five. Seventeen-ten hours exactly. I've got four hours before they come for me. So here goes.

This all started six days ago.

Six days ago, on Thursday.

THURSDAY

1

The Dreaded Question

I chewed on my pencil, deep in thought. Mr Oakley was only three away from asking me the dreaded question. What was I going to say?

'Your turn, Ann. What does your mum do for a living?' asked Mr Oakley.

I switched my pencil from one side of my mouth to the other and carried on chewing. I gazed out of the classroom window in a bit of a wistful haze – I admit it!

. . . My mum's a squadron leader in the SAS. She rescued the Prime Minister when he was kidnapped a few months ago and no-one ever heard about it 'cause Mum was on a top secret mission.

'My mum can't find a job, sir. She's on the dole,' Ann replied to the teacher's question.

One down, two more to go. And then . . .

'And you, Shula? What about your mum? What does she do?' asked Mr Oakley.

I drifted back into my daydream again,

13

answering the teacher's question in my head.

My mum's about to be signed up by Arsenal football club. She's going to be their first ever woman centre forward . . .

'Mum works at the BBC. She produces radio programmes for the radio,' Shula preened.

'Well, she wouldn't produce radio programmes for the TV, would she?' Harrison muttered from beside me. 'Rotten poser!'

Harrison (or Nosh as everyone calls him) wasn't the only one muttering under his breath. Everyone in the class had heard about Shula's mum and her job and the mega amounts of money she got paid and the stars she'd had lunch with – until we were all sick up to the eyebrows of hearing it!

'She gets really well paid and she . . .'

'Yes, Shula. I think we get the idea,' said Mr Oakley, moving on quickly. 'Your turn, Nosh. What does your mum do?'

I smiled – miles away – as I considered another possibility.

My mum's going to be the first person on Mars. Her spaceship leaves from Brighton tomorrow morning at dawn . . .

Yeah . . . That's what my mum should do. If only . . .

'Sir, my mum says she's a domestic technical engineer,' Nosh said proudly.

My ears pricked up. That sounded interesting. I didn't know Nosh's mum did anything like that.

'Oh, yes? What's a domestic technical engineer?' Mr Oakley asked.

'It's what's otherwise known as a housewife!' Nosh grinned.

The rest of the class tittered. I elbowed Nosh in the ribs for being such a twerp!

'But Mum says she prefers the fancy title!' Nosh added.

'Hhmm!' Mr Oakley smiled but said nothing else. He turned to me. I swallowed hard. My turn now. What should I say? How could I put it so that it'd be exciting, interesting, *world-shattering* . . .

'Elliot?' Mr Oakley prompted.

'Yes, sir?'

'Your mum?' asked the teacher. 'What does she do for a living?'

'My mum . . .' I sighed inwardly. My voice lowered with dejection. 'Mum's a secretary.'

'Good!' Already Mr Oakley was moving on to the next person.

I slumped in my chair, my head resting on my cupped hand.

A secretary!

That was about as interesting as stale bread. I scowled, imagining Mum's face before me. As soon as I got home I was going to have to speak to Mum about changing her job! She should be doing something more adventurous, something more . . . exciting!

Now that he'd asked the entire class, Mr Oakley started dribbling on about the various roles women played in the current economy compared to centuries past. It was a close-run thing, but even the lesson was probably more interesting than Mum's job! I decided that when I got home, Mum and I were definitely going to have a serious talk!

2

Elliot, You're Cute!

'You're not watching that, are you?' Mum flopped down onto the sofa and reached for the remote control. Without waiting for my reply she switched TV channels.

'Mum! Yes, I was watching that film actually,' I spluttered.

'But the news is on.' Mum settled back against the cushions, kicked off her shoes and studied the TV screen intently.

'Mum!' I said, annoyed.

'Yes, dear?'

I sighed with impatience. Every evening when Mum came home it was always the same thing. We'd have dinner, she'd work for an hour on her PC, then she'd plonk herself down on the sofa, kick off her shoes and flick over until she came to a channel – somewhere – that was showing the news.

'Mum – the film?' I tried again, knowing I was fighting a losing battle.

'Just a minute, Elliot. I want to see what's happening in the world,' said Mum.

'But it's so depressing.'

'And watching that film with people being shot at left, right and centre isn't?' asked Mum.

'At least the film isn't real.'

'Elliot, you're cute, but you should take more notice of what's going on in the world around you.'

I slumped back in my chair. 'Mum, I wish you wouldn't call me that . . .'

'Call you what?'

'Cute!' I said with disgust. 'You're always telling me I'm cute. And yesterday you called me that in front of Nosh.'

'But you are cute, Elliot,' Mum smiled.

'Mum . . .'

'OK! OK! I won't show you up in public any more. But only if I can still call you cute in private.' Mum grinned.

I shook my head. Mum was definitely in one of her funny-peculiar moods!

'Why don't you go for a walk or something?' Mum suggested. 'You could do with the exercise.'

'I'm fit enough, thank you,' I sulked.

'I think I should buy you a dog for your birthday.' Mum carried on as if I hadn't spoken. 'At least that way you'd have to go to the park every day and get some fresh air, instead of staring at the TV or my PC screen all the time.'

'The park! You must be joking. You know how much I hate the park.'

'Why? What's wrong with it? I used to love going to the park when I was your age.' Mum looked all wistful. 'I used to love the children's playground – especially the swings. They were my favourite. What's your favourite part of the park?'

'Tony's Fish and Chip shop across the road!' I replied.

Mum laughed. 'Honestly, Elliot! What am I going to do with you?'

'Let me watch the rest of the film?' I tried.

'After the news.' Mum said. Then she looked up at the clock on the wall. 'Wait a minute. Is that the time? You couldn't have seen the end of that film anyway. It's getting close to your bedtime.'

That was it! The battle was well and truly lost! Mum turned up the volume as a presenter on the TV stood with a microphone in her hand, facing the camera.

'*Today, the environmental pressure group ANTIDOTE – or Action Now Thwarts Immoral Destruction Of The Environment – launched another demonstration against the chemical company, Shelby and Pardela Pharmaceuticals.*

The chief executive of ANTIDOTE, Sarah Irving, insisted that ANTIDOTE have acquired information proving that Shelby and Pardela are experimenting on rare and exotic animals, smuggled illegally into this country. I asked the co-chairman of Shelby's, Mr Marcus Pardela, for his comments on these allegations.'

The scene cut to Marcus Pardela himself, a tall, broad man in a dark blue suit entering the Shelby and Pardela building. He was asked something which was lost under the commentary of some other wittering journalist, something which obviously made him angry. He turned to the camera, his eyes blazing.

'I've never heard such arrant nonsense. And what's more, I shall be contacting my lawyers and instructing them to sue Sarah Irving and her so-called protest organization ANTIDOTE for slander. My company has never and will never use rare animals in experiments. At the very least Sarah Irving has been misinformed. Now if you'll excuse me.' And with that, Marcus Pardela pushed past the reporters surrounding him and entered the building.

I couldn't help smiling. My Uncle Robert worked for ANTIDOTE and he was always moaning about the way the TV and the newspapers reported his organization's activities. That last report was bound to have him complaining about how Marcus Pardela and not ANTIDOTE was given the last word.

'What d'you think of that?' Mum asked me.

'Of what?'

'That news item about ANTIDOTE.'

'Uncle will be pleased to see ANTIDOTE in the news again,' I shrugged.

'I didn't mean that. I was talking about ANTIDOTE demonstrating against Shelby and Pardela Pharmaceuticals,' Mum continued.

I frowned at her, surprised at the question. 'It's got nothing to do with me.'

Mum shook her head. 'Yes, it does, Elliot. We each have to take responsibility for the world we live in.'

'But I can't do much about it,' I protested.

'Why not?'

'I'm just a kid.'

'So how old do you have to be before you can make a difference?' Mum asked.

'I don't know. Besides, one person can't really make that much of a difference, can they?' I shrugged.

'Elliot, one person can make a lot of difference. All the difference in the world. I've told you that often enough,' Mum said urgently.

I wrinkled up my nose. Mum and I had argued about this so many times before and I really didn't want to discuss it again. Mum seemed to think that I could set off in the morning, move Mount Everest to Australia all by myself and be home in time for dinner – all I had to do was want it enough!

'Mum, why are you a secretary?' I asked, remembering my lesson earlier.

Mum turned to look at me. She had a strange, wary frown on her face. 'Why shouldn't I be?'

'But you've told me you weren't always a secretary.'

'So?'

'So what did you do before?'

'A bit of this. A bit of that . . .'

'What does that mean?' It was like trying to get blood out of a stone!

'It means it's time for your bed,' Mum said decisively.

'Just tell me what you did before you were a secretary and then I'll go to bed,' I cajoled.

'Elliot, some other time. I'm very tired,' Mum sighed. 'Now off you go and clean your teeth – and try cleaning the ones at the back of your mouth as well as the ones at the front. They need love and attention too.'

I stood up and walked slowly to the living-room door before turning back to Mum. A deep frown crept across my face. I'd only just realized something.

'Why is it that whenever I ask you about

what you did before you were a secretary, you always change the subject and try to shut me up?'

'I don't.' Mum raised her eyebrows.

'Oh, yes you do. You always do it.'

'You're imagining things.'

'I don't think so.'

Mum studied me, then sighed again. 'If you must know, I used to work for the government.'

'Doing what?' I moved closer.

'Special operations.'

'What does that mean?' Whatever it was, it sounded really exciting.

'It means I signed the Official Secrets Act so I'm not supposed to talk about it,' Mum replied. 'I'm not trying to be deliberately vague. It's just I'm not meant to discuss it, even with my son.'

I walked back into the room and sat down on the arm of the sofa. Mum didn't shout at me to sit down properly the way she usually did.

'Was it something top secret and exciting and dangerous?' I asked, hopefully.

'No, dear,' Mum laughed. 'It was dull and tedious and very boring. That's why I left. I had to retrieve and file documents mostly.'

My shoulders slumped with disappoint-ment. 'Oh, is that all?'

'Yep! That's all. Now off you go, Elliot.' Mum smiled. 'I'll be up in a minute.'

I left the room and trudged up the stairs. All things considered, I knew I should be grateful that Mum at least had a job. A lot of my friends had parents who were out of work. But I must admit, I couldn't help thinking, *wishing* – if only . . .

3

Uncle Robert

I reached the landing when the doorbell rang. I turned round to answer it but Mum beat me to it.

'It's OK. You go and clean your teeth,' Mum called up to me.

But I hung around. I wanted to see who it was first. Mum opened the door.

'Uncle Robert!' I dashed down the stairs. 'Hi, Uncle Robert. How're you doing?'

'How am I doing what?' Uncle Robert grinned.

I laughed, even though Uncle Robert always says that when I ask him how he's doing. 'I didn't know you were back in the country. When did you arrive? What were you working on this time? Was it exciting? Did you . . . ?'

'Er . . . Elliot, that's enough. Your bed is calling to you. Your questions will have to wait till the next time Uncle Robert comes round,' said Mum.

'But . . .'

'Don't worry, Elliot. I'll be round at the weekend and then I'll tell you all about it. In the meantime, I've got you a present,' winked Uncle Robert.

'You have? Great!' I looked at Uncle's hands which were both empty. 'Where is it?'

'Elliot!' Mum frowned.

I know I was being a bit what I would call eager and Mum would call rude, but presents are presents! Uncle Robert tilted back his head and roared with laughter. He dug into his inside jacket pocket and brought out an envelope. He went to hand over the envelope, but snatched it back before I'd barely touched it.

'Have you still got all the other games I've brought you?' asked Uncle Robert.

'Of course.'

'Finished them?'

'Naturally!'

What a question! Of course I'd finished them! Mum wasn't the only one in the family who could find her way around a computer. In fact sometimes – well, just occasionally when she was playing one of my games! – she had to ask me how to do things.

'You won't finish this one,' said Uncle Robert confidently. 'This game is my best one ever.'

'What kind is it?' I jumped up and snatched the envelope out of Uncle's hand. I tore it open. It contained three 3.5 inch disks labelled Elliot-1, Elliot-2, Elliot-3.

'I'm not telling you that. That's for you to find out – hot shot!' Uncle laughed.

'But not now,' said Mum quickly. 'You can find out tomorrow night after you've done your homework.'

'But can't I even . . .'

'No, Elliot. I mean it,' said Mum firmly.

Mum had that glinty, steely look in her eyes. I knew better than to argue.

'Oh, all right.' I turned to Uncle Robert. 'Thanks for the game. I can't wait to try it.'

I began to run up the stairs, before I remembered something. 'Uncle Robert, what's it called?'

'Huh?'

'The game?'

Uncle Robert considered for a moment. 'You've got to find that out,' he said at last. 'That's the whole point of the game.'

I raised my eyebrows. 'That's different.'

'Good night, Elliot.' Uncle Robert smiled.

''Night, Uncle. 'Night, Mum.' And off I went to clean my teeth.

I gave my mouth a quick final rinse before straightening up to check my teeth in the mirror before me. I was surprised and then not surprised to find myself frowning. What kind of game was it where the point of the game was to find out the *name* of the game? I'd never heard of that one before – but I liked it! I admit it, I was intrigued. Uncle Robert designed and programmed games for me in his spare time and I loved it. To have a game designed just for me was so . . . *choice*! And my friends at school were always impressed too. It also meant that I was in every one. In each game, the hero of the story was a boy called Elliot! So far Uncle Robert had designed three different games for me, each one harder than the last. I'd battled dinosaurs, fought my way past dragons and rescued colonists on a doomed planet. I couldn't wait to see what Uncle Robert had in store for me this time. But I couldn't for the life of me figure out how the game might work. If I quickly loaded it up now, I could at least check the game's format. That wouldn't take *too* long . . .

It was no good! I just had to load it up now. I couldn't wait till the morning to see what kind of game it was. I'd use Mum's computer but I'd have to be careful that Mum didn't catch me – not after she'd told me to go straight to bed. I knew if Mum caught me she would go ballistic to say the least, but I couldn't help it. I was desperate to try it out. I tiptoed out of the bathroom and across the landing to my bedroom to get the disks.

'I'll only be on Mum's PC for five minutes. Just five minutes,' I muttered, already working out my excuses in case Mum caught me.

But I didn't make it to my bedroom. Raised voices reached me from downstairs. I stopped and looked over the banister. I couldn't believe it, but Mum and Uncle Robert were *arguing*. I'd never, *ever* heard them argue before. I crept down the stairs. Mum and Uncle Robert were in the living room and the door was shut but as I reached the hall, snatches of their conversation echoed out to me.

'ANTIDOTE needs your help, Lisa. I need your help. *Please!*' Uncle Robert's voice was a mixture of frustration and entreaty.

' . . . No! *No! NO!* How many more times?' Mum replied furiously. 'I gave all that up when Elliot was born. I'm not getting back into it now.'

'But we need you . . .'

'So does Elliot. No!'

'If I do this job alone, I'll be found out in less than a minute,' said Uncle Robert. 'You're the expert, not me.'

'Expert? Yeah, right! What did it ever get me? Nothing. And where did it ever get me?

Nowhere. I'm not doing it, Robert, and that's final.' Mum's voice was bitter.

Stunned, I moved in closer towards the living-room door.

'Just look at the data on this disk – that's all I ask,' Uncle Robert pleaded.

'Why? I won't change my mind,' said Mum.

'Lisa, this data is important. It was smuggled out of Shelby's two days ago,' Uncle Robert began.

'I'm not interested.'

I recognized Mum's tone. When she was in that kind of mood, nothing short of a ton of dynamite could shift her.

'Lisa, they *are* performing experiments on illegally imported, rare animals in that building. It goes on in their top-security lab down in the basement. This data refers to it – but it's not enough. Someone needs to get into Shelby's and film what's going on,' said Uncle Robert.

'I'm not doing it, Robert. And you have no right to ask me.' Mum's voice was so low, I had to strain to hear it.

'Lisa, listen. There's . . . there's something else. Some of us at ANTIDOTE have found out that Shelby's have planted an agent in our organization,' said Uncle Robert. 'We managed to get a print-out of a confidential memo, written by Marcus Pardela himself where he talks about his "mole" in our group.'

At Mum's stunned gasp, I pressed my ear right up against the cool wooden door.

'An agent? Are you sure?' Mum asked.

'Positive. Someone at ANTIDOTE is secretly working for Shelby's. I was hoping you'd help us find out who, once this other business is out of the way. Please say you'll help us. We can't call in someone from outside in case the news leaks out and damages our organization and we can't tell too many people in the organization what's going on in case our "mole" goes underground,' said Uncle Robert. 'I wouldn't ask you to do this if I didn't desperately need you – you know that.'

'You don't want much, do you?' Mum said tersely.

Silence.

'Who else knows about this confidential letter about the mole?' asked Mum.

'Just me, Sarah Irving – she's chief executive of ANTIDOTE, Ian Macmillan, the general secretary and Rohan Adjava, the treasurer. Four people – that's it. And the other three are as anxious as I am to find out who's betraying us to Shelby's. But we've all agreed that getting proof of Shelby's experiments on illegally imported animals is our first priority.'

'Let me see the letter about this so-called agent,' Mum said.

I straightened up. What on earth was going on? Why did Uncle Robert need Mum's help? What kind of help? What could Mum do? Uncle Robert called her 'the expert'. What did that mean? The expert in what? My head was like a beehive, buzzing with questions. It was all quiet in the living room now. I turned to head back to my bedroom and knocked into the hall table. It rocked against the wall with a loud thud. In the next moment, I legged it up the stairs. I was only halfway up when the living-room door opened. Thinking quickly, I turned and ran down the stairs just as Mum and Uncle Robert came out of the living room.

'Hi! I'm just coming down for some water,' I said.

'And then straight to bed – OK?'

I nodded, noting the sheet of paper in Mum's hand, the serious look on both the grown-ups' faces.

'So when are you coming to see us next, Uncle?' I asked.

'On Sunday, bright and early. You can both spend the day with me,' Uncle Robert replied.

'Brill!' I started up the stairs again.

'I thought you wanted a drink of water?' said Mum.

'Oh, yeah.' I could feel my face growing hot. What a giveaway!

Ignoring the slight yet knowing smile on Mum's face, I went into the kitchen. I poured myself half a glass of ice-cold water from the fridge and downed it in one. Then I headed back to my bedroom. Mum and Uncle Robert stood in the hall watching me go up the stairs.

'Elliot, you're cute, but if I catch you eavesdropping at this door, you're in trouble!' said Mum.

'As if!' I called down from the landing.

'Yeah, right!' Mum followed Uncle Robert back into the living room, shutting the door firmly behind her.

FRIDAY

4

The Long Run

'Why've you got a face like a handful of mince?' Nosh frowned. 'Anyone would think it was Monday morning instead of Friday evening. School's over for the next three weeks. We're on holiday. What more do you want? Blood?'

I sat back on Nosh's sofa, but I couldn't relax. It was past nine and we'd had a brilliant dinner of pepperoni pizza because Nosh's mum was at the cinema with her friends so Nosh's dad had sent out for a meal. Here I was, next door at Nosh's house playing one of my favourite video games, and was I enjoying it? No, not much! All I had on my mind was Mum and the strange conversation I'd heard the night before.

When I'd got home earlier, Mum told me I was spending the night at Nosh's house. She didn't ask if I wanted to, she just told me. Mind you, usually I couldn't wait to stay over with Nosh. We'd spend all night reading comics or playing games by torchlight – but I didn't want to do it, not this time. This time, I was sure it was just a ploy on Mum's part to get me out of the way. When I'd asked Mum where she was going, all she said was, 'Your Uncle Robert and I have some things to sort out – that's why I can't be here. And I'm not leaving you on your own.'

'Why can't you sort out whatever it is from here?' I asked.

'It's not that simple,' Mum sighed. 'Don't argue with me, Elliot – not tonight. Please?'

Mum looked tired and kind of worried, so I shut up. Against my better judgement, I packed up my stuff and headed next door to Nosh's house.

The only trouble was, I'd spent every minute since then thinking about what Mum and Uncle Robert might be up to.

I looked at Nosh, wondering if I should confide in my best friend. I sighed for the umpteenth time in ten minutes. I couldn't help it! All this wondering and worrying was driving me crazy.

'What's the matter, Elliot?' Nosh asked impatiently. 'Tell me before I have to kill you! All your sighing and moping about is really starting to cheese me off.'

'It's about Uncle Robert and Mum,' I began slowly. 'I think Uncle Robert is trying to get Mum to do something that'll get her into trouble.'

'What kind of trouble?' Nosh's ears pricked up at once. That's the thing about Nosh. He loves to know everyone's business.

'I'm not sure,' I admitted.

'This isn't another of your worry wart ideas, is it?' Nosh asked suspiciously.

'What d'you mean?'

'Well, you must admit,' Nosh said, 'sometimes you'll get an idea in your head and worry it to death.'

'Rubbish!' I said indignantly. 'My mum's up to something – or at least she might be.'

'I'm still waiting for you to tell me what kind of something,' said Nosh.

I took a deep breath. 'Well, it's like this . . .' I began.

And I relayed the whole of the conversation I'd heard between Mum and Uncle Robert the night before. By the time I'd finished, Nosh looked just as perplexed as I felt – which, I must admit, did make me feel a bit better.

'Is that all true?' Nosh asked.

'Of course it's true,' I snapped. 'I wouldn't make up something like that.'

'ANTIDOTE . . . Halle's always going on about them,' Nosh mused. 'So what does it mean?'

'I wish I knew. But I'm worried. I don't know what went on after I had to go to bed. Maybe Uncle Robert managed to persuade Mum to help him get into the Shelby building and film the experiments on those animals, after all?'

'Wow! Your mum?!' Nosh was as stunned by the idea as I was.

'Maybe I'm worrying about nothing,' I said hopefully.

'It wouldn't be the first time,' Nosh pointed out.

Before I could argue, the doorbell rang. At my look of query, Nosh sniffed with disgust. 'It's probably one of Halle's butt-ugly boyfriends!'

I'd heard all about Nosh's sister's boyfriends. According to Nosh, his sister Halle always chose to go out with boys who Nosh was guaranteed to loathe! Halle's current one scored zero out of ten for patting Nosh on his head the first time they'd met!

'Elliot, could you come here for a moment?' Nosh's dad called out from the hall moments later. It's strange but looking back, that was the moment that changed my life. I can see that now. I only wish I could've seen it then, but I didn't.

I did as requested, followed by Nosh. I

thought it was Mum, back already from wherever it was that she'd had to go. I was wrong.

It was the police.

A man and woman stood at the door, both of them in uniform. The man had light brown hair and the woman was a blonde who looked past Nosh's dad straight at me.

'Elliot Gaines?' said the blond police-woman.

I nodded, swallowing hard. My mind went blank – completely and totally blank.

'Mrs Carlisle, your other next-door neigh-bour, told us we might find you here. Can we talk to you for a moment, son?' the woman continued.

I walked forward slowly, my legs suddenly filled with lead weights.

'Do you know where your mother is, Elliot?' asked the policeman seriously.

I shook my head.

'Has there been an accident?' asked Nosh's dad.

My head snapped around. Even though I'd been thinking the exact same thing, it was still shocking to hear it put into words like that. At that moment, I almost hated Nosh's dad.

'Do you know where your mum is?' the policeman asked me again, ignoring Nosh's dad completely.

'No, I don't.' My voice was little more than a squeak.

'What's this all about, officer?' asked Nosh's dad.

I'll say one thing for him, he was persistent.

'Can I talk to you alone for a moment, sir?' said the policewoman.

Nosh's dad frowned. He stepped out into the front path, pulling the door partially to behind him. Nosh and I immediately moved forward to have a listen.

'Are you any relation to Lisa Gaines?' asked the policewoman.

'No, but we're the best of friends. Elliot's staying here with us until she gets back,' Nosh's dad answered.

'I see.' Now it was the turn of the policeman to speak. In hushed tones, he said, 'Well, Mrs Lisa Gaines and her brother-in-law Robert Gaines were filmed breaking into Shelby and Pardela Pharmaceuticals earlier tonight. Robert Gaines has now been apprehended, but Mrs Gaines is still on the run.'

'Excuse me? I . . . I don't b-believe it. There must be some mistake,' spluttered Nosh's dad.

'No mistake, sir,' the policeman said. 'Mrs Gaines can be seen clearly on the company's security video tape. She's already been identified.'

Nosh turned towards me. I think he said something but I could only see his lips move. No sound came out – at least, none that I could hear. I couldn't understand where that roaring noise in my head was coming from. It was as if I was drowning – floundering in a nightmare, sinking beneath his stare of disbelief and sympathy and suspicion.

As the police and Nosh's dad stepped back into the house, Nosh and I bounded back. I don't know about Nosh but I was functioning on auto-pilot.

'If your mum does phone you, Elliot, or if she tries to get in touch, please let us know,' the policewoman said. 'She's in trouble and you must tell her to give herself up. She's not doing herself any good by going on the run like this and sooner or later we're going to catch her. It would look better for her in the long run if she gave herself up to us first before that happens.'

'My mum didn't break into Shelby and Whatsit or anywhere else,' I shouted. The words exploded from me in a burst of white-hot anger. 'I heard what you said to Nosh's dad and it's a *lie*.'

The policewoman opened her mouth to argue, only to snap it shut again. 'Just tell her to give herself up if she tries to get in touch with you,' she repeated. 'OK, Elliot?'

No, it wasn't OK. What a stupid thing to say. *The police were after Mum*. For something she hadn't done. For something she *couldn't* have done. It was ridiculous, outrageous. But here they were knocking on the door and asking for her.

'What's going to happen to my uncle?' I asked.

'He'll be remanded on bail, then allowed to go back home, I suppose,' the policeman said. 'It's really up to the magistrate, though.'

As Nosh's dad closed the door behind the two policemen, Nosh turned to me, his eyes huge with delighted disbelief.

'Your mum's not really on the run, is she?' he asked. 'Did she really break into Shelby's?'

I scowled at him.

'Nosh, that's enough,' Nosh's dad said firmly. 'Leave him alone. Elliot, you're welcome to stay with us until your mother comes home and this business is all cleared up. I'm sure the police have just made a stupid mistake.'

'They didn't seem to think so,' Nosh muttered.

'Nosh, you're not helping,' his dad pointed out impatiently.

Nosh took a quick look at my stormy face and he had the grace to look contrite. 'Sorry!' he muttered again.

'Elliot, d'you know anything about this?' Nosh's dad questioned.

After a quick glance at Nosh, I shook my head. It was the truth in a way. I hadn't a clue. What did the police say? Uncle Robert had been arrested? Was he the one who'd identified Mum on the video tape? OK, so they'd talked about getting into the Shelby building – but Mum wouldn't have done that. She *couldn't*. She was just a secretary. What did she know about all that 'James Bond' stuff? My head was swimming with questions and one thing was for sure, I wouldn't find any answers in Nosh's house.

'I'd better go home now,' I said.

'I don't think that's a very good idea . . .' Nosh's dad began.

'I'm only going to get some more clothes – if I'm going to stay here for a while . . .' I said quickly.

'Of course you are. You can't stay in your house all by yourself, can you?' said Nosh's dad.

Actually, that was exactly what I wanted to do, but I knew Nosh's dad would cut up rough about it if I argued.

'I won't be long,' I said, heading for the front door.

'You'll be right back?' asked Nosh's dad.

'I'll be right back.'

'D'you want me to come with you?' asked Nosh's dad.

I shook my head. I wanted to be alone. I had a lot to think about.

'Hang on a sec, Elliot,' said Nosh. 'I'll come with you.'

'No, that's all right . . .'

'No problem,' Nosh insisted.

I glared at Nosh, irritated. Nosh could be just as stubborn as his dad. Why wouldn't either of them take the broad hint and leave me alone? I didn't want to be around them or anyone else for that matter. I opened the front door and headed down the garden path as quickly as I could. It wasn't quick enough. Nosh was right behind me.

'You don't have to come with me, you know. I think I can make it from your house to mine without getting lost,' I snapped.

'It's no trouble,' Nosh shrugged.

With a deep, obvious sigh, I made my way up my own garden path. I opened the front door without a word and walked in, choosing to ignore Nosh completely. I'd barely taken a step when I stopped abruptly and listened. The house felt so strange, so *empty*. There were often times when I was in the house by myself, when Mum was late from work or was out shopping, but the house had never felt like this before. I supposed it was because I always knew that Mum was safe and coming back home soon. But not this time. This time, she was in trouble.

'Your mum will be all right, Elliot. I know she will.'

I started at Nosh's voice behind me. To be honest, I'd forgotten that he was there.

'I'd better go and get my stuff,' I said quietly.

I made my way upstairs to my bedroom. The envelope containing the three disks my uncle had given me sat conspicuously on my bedside table. I hadn't even had the chance to load them up on to Mum's PC and see what was on them yet. It was almost as if I'd been given them in another lifetime, another world – a sane, normal world where Uncle Robert was just an ordinary uncle and Mum . . . Mum wasn't on the run from the police . . . I picked up the envelope and fingered it absentmindedly. I had to do something. I had to find out what was happening. But where should I start? Just at that moment, the phone downstairs rang. I spun around, almost knocking Nosh flying, and raced out of the room down the stairs, stuffing the envelope into my trouser pocket as I ran.

Let it be Mum. Please let it be Mum.

'Hello? Hello?' I panted into the phone.

'Elliot? Thank goodness! Are you all right?'

'Mum!' I clutched the phone tighter. Behind me I was only just aware of Nosh's gasp. 'Mum, where are you? What's going on? Mum, the police . . .'

'Elliot, all that'll have to wait,' Mum interrupted. 'I need you to do something for me – and you can't tell anyone, not even Nosh.'

'What is it?' I asked breathlessly.

As Nosh moved in closer, I turned my back on him. Usually I didn't mind his nosiness. Now I did.

'I want you to get my personal organizer from the top drawer of my bedside table and keep it in a safe place until tomorrow. I'll phone you tomorrow at precisely nine-fifteen in the morning. I'll let you know then where the two of us can meet.'

'But Mum, the police are after you. They told me to let them know if you phoned me or tried to get in contact with me.'

'Are you going to?'

'Of course not,' I said, shocked.

I heard Mum chuckle down the phone. 'Elliot, you are just the cutest! What would I do without you?'

Yet despite Mum's light, seemingly jovial tone, I could tell it was an act put on for my benefit. There was no mistaking the edge to her voice.

'Mum, please tell me what's going on,' I

begged. 'They say you broke into Shelby and Whatsit with Uncle Robert and that they have both of you filmed on a security video tape . . .'

'Do you believe them?'

'NO!' The word exploded from me like an ICBM. 'Of course I don't. But what about the security tape . . . ?'

'Elliot, that tape is a fake, I promise you,' Mum said seriously. 'There's no way they have a tape showing me breaking into Shelby's.'

'Then why can't you just go to the police and tell them that?'

'It's not that simple.'

'But if you didn't do it . . .' It seemed that simple to me. Perfectly simple.

'Elliot, I'll explain when I see you. In the meantime keep my organizer somewhere very, *very* safe,' said Mum. 'And don't tell anyone about our conversation. Not Nosh, not the police, and especially not anyone from ANTIDOTE.'

'Is that because someone there is working for Shelby's?' I asked.

'I *knew* you were listening at the door, you nosy hound! You're as bad as your friend Nosh,' said Mum. There was a sudden clatter at the other end of the line, as if Mum had dropped the phone.

'Mum? MUM?'

'Elliot, I have to go now,' Mum said with breathless haste. 'You be very careful. I'll try and sort all this out as soon as possible and don't go to your uncle's house – it isn't safe.'

'Mum, don't go yet . . .'

'I have to. Elliot, until you hear from me – trust no-one.'

'Mum . . .' But the phone purred continuously at me. She'd gone.

'Elliot . . .' Nosh began uncertainly.

I clutched the phone even tighter, willing Mum to pick up her phone again and call me. It didn't happen. I slammed the phone down on the receiver and glared at it.

'Elliot . . .'

'Nosh, bog off and leave me alone,' I fired at him.

Nosh seemed to shrink into himself. He gave me a look as if I was something really unpleasant he'd just stepped in. Then, without a word, he turned and headed for the front door. He'd opened it before I cooled down enough to speak.

'Sorry, Nosh – OK?'

Silence.

'I'm sorry. I've just . . . I've just got a lot on my mind.'

'I'd figured that out for myself,' Nosh replied dryly.

'If you really want to help, you won't ask me

to tell you what Mum said. And you won't tell your mum and dad that I've even spoken to her,' I told him.

'You've got it!' said Nosh.

I smiled at him gratefully. 'Come on, then,' I said. 'But no questions – OK?'

'I promise.'

But I couldn't get over the feeling that soon I was going to need not just Nosh's help, but all the help I could get.

5

Password Protected

Mum's personal organizer was just where she said it'd be.

'What's that, then?' asked Nosh, forgetting that he wasn't supposed to ask any questions.

'It's Mum's personal organizer,' I replied.

Nosh moved in for a closer look. 'Her what?'

'It's like a pocket computer,' I explained. 'Mum usually takes it everywhere she goes.'

Which of course didn't explain why she'd suddenly left it behind tonight. Usually you couldn't prise Mum's organizer out of her hands with a crowbar. Mum always said she wouldn't be able to find our house if she didn't have her organizer on her!

'Show us how it works, then,' said Nosh.

I opened the organizer and pressed the <ON> button.

'I don't know Mum's password so I've never been able to get any further than this,' I admitted.

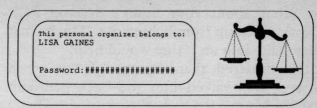

```
This personal organizer belongs to:
LISA GAINES

Password: ##################
```

'That's a fat lot of good.' Nosh was not impressed. 'So what does your mum keep on it, then?'

'She says it's just a few addresses and telephone numbers, and a couple of documents that she's writing.'

'Then why all the secrecy?'

'Mum thinks I'm nosy enough already without encouraging me to snoop on her organizer.' I looked at Nosh pointedly. 'She must be confusing me with you.'

'Bloomin' cheek!' Nosh snorted. 'I'm not nosy. I'm just interested in things, that's all.'

'Yeah, right!'

I pressed the <OFF> key and, closing the lid of the organizer, I slipped it into my right trouser pocket. It was the safest place I could think of for the moment. Then I looked around the room – Mum's room. I don't know what I was hoping for. Maybe I expected a piece of paper to drift down from the ceiling with *EXPLANATION* written in big, black letters across the top! Anyway, it didn't happen.

'What about your mum's desktop PC?' Nosh piped up from behind me. 'Maybe that has some info on it that would help.'

I considered, then shrugged. It was worth a try. We walked into the back bedroom which Mum used as her work room. There, on a large pedestal table against one wall, was Mum's multimedia PC. To be honest, I was really proud of Mum's machine. It was a lot better than the ones we have at school. It not only played all sorts of CDs but it even let you play videos straight from a camcorder or a VCR – and you could edit the videos as well. What's more, you could get TV channels on it, but Mum had disconnected that facility. She said she didn't want to encourage me to watch even more TV than I did already, especially when I should be doing my homework. Next to the screen was a scanner which looked a bit like a small photocopier. All you had to do was put in a document, a page at a time and the information was automatically transferred to a file or the screen which meant you didn't have to type the whole document again. The scanner could even store photographic images in files on the computer. Mum's PC also allowed whole documents to be recorded by dictating them using a microphone linked to the processor. Messages and mail could be sent via the modem to any other computer which also had a modem attached, and Mum was on the Internet. In fact Mum said the only thing her machine couldn't do was make the beds and that was just a matter of time!

'We'd better make this fast before Dad comes knocking on the door to find out where we are,' Nosh warned.

I switched on the machine and sat down. Nosh dragged a chair next to mine and we watched as the machine booted up. In less than a minute, we were into the word processor and a file called ANTI-DOTE.CONFIDENTIAL. The file came up automatically, so it was obviously the last thing Mum had been working on.

'This must be the memo that Uncle Robert gave to Mum,' I said. 'Mum must've scanned it into the computer.'

Nosh and I both leaned forward for a closer look.

```
SHELBY AND PARDELA PHARMACEUTICALS

Electronic Memo: Page 1 of 1

To:     Joshua Shelby - JSHELBY
From:   Marcus Pardela - MPARDELA
cc:
Status: Strictly Confidential
```

Nosh and I looked at each other.

'So it's really true. Someone at ANTI-
DOTE *is* working for Shelby's. I'll print out
this letter so that we have a copy of it,' I said,
hitting the <Print Screen> key.

'But how do we find out who? And how
does that help us find out what's going on with
your mum? And how will we . . . ?'

I raised my hand to stop Nosh's questions.
I didn't have any immediate answers any
more than he did and I didn't like feeling so
feeble. I picked up the print-out of the memo
and studied it again.

'I wonder what that bit means?'

'Which bit?'

'"Just remember whose idea all this was in
the first place . . ."' I pointed to the relevant
section of the letter.

56

'Hhmm! No idea.' Nosh shook his head.

'It's a strange thing to say. I wonder what idea he's talking about?' I mused.

'We'll never know,' shrugged Nosh. 'And besides, that's not the important bit of the memo. What's important is, you have *proof* about the Shelby agent.'

'So now what? We must do something,' I said, frustrated.

'Like?' Nosh sat back, his arms folded across his chest as he waited for me to answer.

'We have to prove that Mum didn't break into Shelby's,' I began.

'How? Do we walk up to Marcus Pardela and demand to see the tape? "Excuse me, Mr Pardela but we want to see the security video you're supposed to have of Elliot's mum. We think you've doctored it in some way and we want to try and prove it,"' Nosh said scornfully.

'Well, the police must have a copy of the tape . . .'

'They're about as likely to show it to us as Marcus Pardela is.'

'Maybe we could get someone at ANTI-DOTE to help us? After all, Uncle Robert works for them,' I thought out loud. 'We could look up their address and phone number in the phone book.'

'And then what? Someone at ANTIDOTE

57

is an agent. A spy! A traitor! And we don't know who. If we go blundering around, we could make things worse for your mum and your uncle – not better.'

'Then what would you suggest?' I asked, annoyed.

That shut him up!

'Yeah, that's what I thought,' I said. Now it was my turn to be less than impressed.

'You're the ideas person in this partnership,' Nosh told me. 'I'm just the voice of logic and reason.'

'Since when?'

'Since five seconds ago!'

I folded up the print-out of the letter and put it in my pocket with Mum's organizer. I came out of Mum's file and had a hunt around the hard disk for anything else that might throw some light on what was going on. Nothing jumped out at me. As far as I could see it was just a load of ordinary-looking data and text files. I didn't really know what I was looking for. To be honest, I wasn't even sure why Mum needed all the PC equipment she had, I was just glad she did. I'd never thought to ask her before. I guess I'd just been too busy enjoying it. And now Mum was missing and I couldn't even ask her – at least not until I spoke to her next. All at once, knowing why Mum had all this stuff seemed terribly important. It was as if I was waking up from a long, long daze and for the first time I was seeing and hearing things that I'd been too preoccupied before to notice.

'Anything?' Nosh asked.

I shook my head. 'Not that I can find. Just lots of files and documents sorted into job numbers. Lots of job numbers.'

'Job numbers?'

'For each different job Mum does, it looks like she holds all the files and documents to do with that job in a different area – and each one of those areas has got a different job number. But I can't tell what any of the jobs are by just having a look at the numbers.'

'Why don't you go into some of the files and have a look?' Nosh suggested.

But before I could answer, the doorbell rang. Nosh and I exchanged a look.

'Dad!'

'Your dad!'

Nosh and I spoke in unison.

'We'd better get going,' Nosh sighed.

I took one last look at the computer screen, then switched everything off. I decided to have a closer, more detailed look the following day after meeting Mum. I ran into my bedroom to shove a few things into a carrier bag whilst Nosh went to the door.

'Elliot, I think you should come over to our

house now,' Nosh's dad called out from the hall. 'We don't want you in here brooding.'

We? Who was 'we'? I shook my head at my reflection in the wardrobe mirror. Nosh's dad sounded just like a grown-up! I noticed that my pockets were bulging so I took out Mum's organizer and Uncle Robert's disks and placed them on top of the carrier bag. I didn't want Nosh's dad asking me questions about what 'we' might have in our pockets! After a moment's thought, I stuffed them down under my clean pair of trousers, balled up at the top of the bag.

My thoughts turned to Uncle Robert. I was slightly ashamed of myself. I'd been so busy concentrating on how Mum was doing and what she was going through that I hadn't really thought about my uncle. Maybe Mum and I could visit him at the police station tomorrow? Maybe with his help we'd get all this straightened out and life could return to normal. With one last look around, I left my bedroom and switched off the light.

As we left the house, Nosh nudged me and indicated across the street with his head. Two men stood watching us. The moment it was obvious we were looking at them as well, they turned and started talking to each other.

'Who're they?' I frowned.

'Must be the police,' Nosh whispered back.

'Maybe they're hoping your mum will turn up tonight and they've been sent to grab her when she does.'

'Or maybe they're just waiting for someone who lives in the house opposite,' I said dryly.

Nosh was getting totally carried away! He always did have a vivid imagination. Much more of an imagination than me.

'No, I reckon I'm right,' Nosh insisted as we headed up his garden path. 'Or maybe they're reporters waiting to do an exclusive story . . .'

'I thought you were meant to be the voice of logic and reason,' I reminded him.

'Oh, yeah! I forgot! In that case, like you said, maybe they're just waiting for someone to come out of the house opposite.' Nosh grinned.

As we walked into Nosh's house, I took one last curious glance back across the street before Nosh's dad shut the door. The two men were both looking my way – watching me intently.

6

Halle

I frowned down at the password screen on Mum's organizer. Why had she wanted me to get hold of this in particular? What was on it? I needed to crack her password and to do that I had to try and think like Mum. What sort of password would she use? I sighed. Knowing Mum it could be anything. I glanced across the room at Nosh who was in his own bed, deep into his *Batman* comic.

Think, Elliot! Think!

I had to work out what the password was – I *had* to. How about 'Nosh is nosy'! No, too short! How about 'Nosh is very nosy'! No. Still too short! Maybe if I . . . Without warning, the door to Nosh's bedroom burst open. I'm surprised it didn't fly off the hinges or at least crash through the wall to fall to the landing on the other side.

Halle stood in the doorway.

And was she cheesed off, or what! She had a expression like a constipated elephant and her whole body was poised like a cobra about to strike.

'You maggot-faced little ratbag!' Completely ignoring me, Halle strode across the room and lifted Nosh bodily out of his bed by his pyjama lapels.

'Dad! DAD!' Nosh yelled at the top of his voice.

'Julian told me what you said about me, you . . . you . . .' Halle released Nosh suddenly and he fell back against his pillows.

I moved cautiously back against the headboard of my own bed as I watched, grateful that I didn't have any older sisters!

'What's the matter?' Nosh's dad called from down the stairs.

'Dad, Halle's trying to kill me!' Nosh shouted.

'Halle, leave your brother alone.' Nosh's dad ran up the stairs. From the sound of it he was taking them two and three at a time. This was obviously something that had happened before.

'D'you know what he told Julian yesterday?' Halle turned to her dad as he entered the room, her eyes still blazing. 'He told Julian that I was trying to find a way to dump him because he had bad breath and BO, but I hadn't told him yet because I wanted to break it to him gently, without hurting his feelings.'

Nosh's dad's lips twitched.

'It's not funny, Dad!' Halle was spitting nails by now.

'No, it's not. Nosh, why did you tell the poor boy that?'

'He deserved it. He *has* got bad breath and BO,' Nosh replied.

Nosh's dad moved like lightning to intercept Halle. Nosh, very wisely, cowered back against the wall. 'Halle, go downstairs and calm down.'

'Yeah, go on. You talk about helping and protecting all creatures? You call yourself *green*?' Nosh taunted.

'Not when it comes to you, you little brat! You're the only exception!' Halle bit out.

'Halle . . .' her dad began.

'Call yourself an ANTIDOTE member? 'Cause I don't.'

'Harrison!' Nosh's dad had that look of 'here we go again' written all over his face. Between the two of them he was definitely fighting a losing battle.

'I should tell ANTIDOTE about you. Get them to throw you out,' Nosh continued.

'ANTIDOTE already know all about you. I told them what a little oik you were when I worked there last summer,' Halle said with satisfaction.

'I bet they didn't believe a word.'

'You wanna bet?'

'Halle, please go downstairs. I'll deal with Nosh,' her dad begged.

'You'd better. If I get my hands on him . . .' Halle threatened. 'You just tell him to keep away from my boyfriends.'

'Why'd I want to hang around your scabby boyfriends?' Nosh asked indignantly. 'I'd rather have my appendix out without an anaesthetic!'

'Dad!' Halle fumed.

'Nosh, shut up – *please*!' Nosh's dad implored.

Halle turned to flounce out of the room. Only then did she notice me.

'Elliot, I don't care if your mum says you are cute – you must be a moron to hang around with my brother!' Halle said scathingly.

A flame of shamed embarrassment shot from my head to my toenails and back up again. Now Halle wasn't the only one who was annoyed!

Just you wait till I see you next, Mum, I silently fumed. How many people had Mum said that to? I'd never be able to hold up my face in our street again!

As Halle marched out of the room, Nosh's dad sighed. 'Nosh, why d'you keep teasing your sister? You know she always rises to the bait, so where's the fun in it?'

'I can't help it, Dad,' said Nosh. 'Halle shouldn't keep picking such dreggy boyfriends, then I'd have nothing to tease her about. And this latest one . . . He's the dregs of the dregs!'

'Was it absolutely necessary to tell him that?' Nosh's dad asked patiently.

'You wouldn't want me to lie about it, would you?'

'No . . . but that doesn't mean you have to volunteer the information either. Just try to be a bit more tactful in future – in the cause of household harmony and my blood pressure, OK?'

'OK, Dad!' Nosh grinned.

Nosh's dad turned to me. 'Are you all right, Elliot? Is there anything I can get you?'

'No, I'm fine thanks,' I replied.

What a lie. I was far from fine. Mum was missing. Uncle Robert was locked up. And watching Nosh and his dad had made me . . . not exactly sad, but kind of wistful. Lots of people say that you can't miss what you've never had – but it's not true. I never really knew my dad. He went to live in Canada when I was less than three years old and I hadn't seen him since. I always thought of him as a tall, shadowy figure whose face I could never quite remember. I've seen photos of course, but it was hard to equate the man in the photos to a real, living, breathing person. At Christmas and on my birthdays he used to phone me. He had a great, deep booming voice like an actor. I remember his voice more than his face and even that I haven't heard in years. He and Mum had a huge, heated quarrel over the phone the last time he called on my birthday. It was all my fault really. When I handed the phone back to Mum, I was in tears. I couldn't understand why he never came to visit me, or why we couldn't go over to Canada to see him. Every time Dad phoned, he promised that next time . . . next time he'd be wishing me Happy Birthday or Merry Christmas in person – but it never happened. I guess Mum must've had enough the last time Dad phoned. She told him that the next time he spoke to me, it'd better be as he promised – in person. That was over two years ago. I hadn't heard from my dad since she'd said that. My dad . . . It's not that I wanted Nosh's dad to be my father. It's just that I sometimes thought how wonderful it would be to have a dad of my own. A dad who was here – especially now.

As Nosh's dad left the room, I buried my feelings before I turned to Nosh.

'I thought you were a goner for sure when Halle leapt across the room at you,' I told him.

'You're not the only one,' Nosh replied dryly.

'And just when did Halle pick up that thing about me being cute?' I remembered, anger flaring through me again.

'Oh, that. It's a joke between your mum and my mum. My mum happened to pass it on, that's all,' said Nosh.

'That was good of her,' I said with disgust.

'You know what mothers are like,' Nosh shrugged.

'Yeah, but your mum doesn't go round showing you up,' I pointed out.

'Yes, she does. She just doesn't tell everyone I'm cute, that's all,' Nosh grinned.

I could see I wasn't going to get much sympathy from him so I turned back to Mum's organizer. I was going to crack this password if it killed me.

An hour later, my eyes felt like they were full of sand and my head kept nodding forwards.

'Elliot, I've just thought of something.' Nosh suddenly lifted his head from his comic. 'According to Halle, ANTIDOTE are holding a protest against Shelby's tomorrow afternoon. Why don't we go and see if we can get to speak to one of the ANTIDOTE bosses? They might know something about your mum and uncle.'

'But I'm going to meet up with Mum

tomorrow morning – remember? She'll tell me what's going on.'

'What if . . . ?' Nosh began.

'What?' I prompted when he didn't continue.

'Nothing.' Nosh shook his head.

I narrowed my eyes suspiciously but he didn't say another word. With a shrug, I returned to Mum's organizer. Frustrated, I snapped the lid shut and buried it under my pillow. I snuggled down and decided to sleep on the problem!

'Hurry up and switch off the light, Nosh,' I said sleepily. 'And good night, Mum – wherever you are.'

The last bit I mouthed silently. It wasn't that I was embarrassed about Nosh hearing me particularly. I just wanted to keep it to myself. As if that way, Mum would sense it or feel it more. 'Take care, Mum,' I whispered again – just to make sure.

Wherever she was, whatever she was doing, I hoped that somehow she knew that I was thinking of her.

SATURDAY

7

Wipe-out

The moment I woke up, I *knew* it was going to be a good day. I could feel it. The sun was already shining bright and warm through my window and the moment my eyes were open, I felt wide awake and alive with the feeling that *things* were going to happen today. Smells of bacon and toast wafted up from downstairs. Another reason to get up! I sprang out of bed, only slowing down slightly when I saw that Nosh was still fast asleep. I dug out my watch which was under my pillow next to Mum's organizer. Eight-thirty. I had forty-five minutes before Mum was going to call. Today this whole business would get sorted out once and for all, and Mum would come home. I felt as if just by thinking it, I could make it happen. The power of positive thinking! Mum would come home and I might even crack her password on her organizer – just for good measure.

I crept out of the room, deciding to have a

shower before doing anything else. After that, I got dressed, then had another crack at Mum's password before going down for my breakfast – and Nosh was *still* asleep!

When Nosh's mum saw me, she said, 'You and Nosh are alike in a lot of things – but not when it comes to getting up in the mornings! I have to scream at him until I'm green, then blue, then purple in the face before he shifts!'

'Nosh and me are alike?' I said, surprised. 'In what way?'

'Just a minute.' Nosh's mum went out into the hall and yelled at the top of her lungs. 'Nosh, out the bed *now* or you can make your own breakfast.' Then she came back into the room.

I sat down at the breakfast table waiting for her to explain. I didn't think Nosh and I were alike at all. In fact, sometimes it surprised me just how well we got on considering that we had so little in common.

'You and Nosh think about things in a similar way. And you both tend to let things get on top of you and then think there's not an awful lot you can do about it. You both give up far too easily.'

I could feel myself getting hotter with every word she spoke. What a load of rubbish!

'That's not true. I don't give up on things . . .'

'I'm not talking about things. I'm talking about giving up on yourself. Your mum says . . .'

'What does my mum say?' I prompted icily when Nosh's mum trailed off.

'Never mind.' Nosh's mum shook her head. 'It was tactless of me to bring up the subject now. I'm sure you've got a lot of other things on your mind. Don't worry about your mum, Elliot. She's just the person to straighten this whole mess out.'

It's amazing how rapidly you can go off some people. Until that moment, I'd always quite liked Nosh's mum. Now she'd plummeted like a lead balloon in my estimation. I glared at her, wondering just what she and Mum had said about me and Nosh.

'Now don't get your boxer shorts in a bunch!' Nosh's mum laughed. 'You look like you're about ready to pounce down my throat.'

I smiled reluctantly, then not so reluctantly when she put a plate of toast, scrambled eggs and bacon in front of me and a huge glass of orange juice.

Nosh didn't put in an appearance until I'd finished my breakfast and my second glass of orange juice. He was in the middle of the longest yawn I'd ever seen. I glanced down at my watch. Ten past nine. I stood up and moved past him.

'See ya, Nosh. I'm popping home for a while,' I told him.

'Why?' Nosh frowned.

'I've got a phone call to . . . make – remember,' I told him pointedly.

'Oh, yeah!' Nosh's eyes opened wide. 'I forgot about that. Hang on a minute. I'll come with you.'

'You can't. You're still in your pyjamas.'

'It'll only take me a minute to change,' Nosh replied.

'Not until you've had a shower, Harrison,' his mum said firmly. 'And Elliot, if you want to make a phone call, you can make it from here. You don't have to go to your house to do it.'

'No, I'd rather. I mean, I want to. I mean . . .' I began to get embarrassed, wondering if I was giving the game away.

'Ah!' Nosh's mum nodded with grown-up understanding. 'Are you going to phone your girlfriend?'

'What girlfriend?' I frowned.

'Don't come over all coy with me.' Nosh's mum wagged her finger. 'I'm sure a cute boy like you has a girlfriend for every day of the week.'

If I heard that word – cute! – one more time . . .

'I'll be back soon,' I told Nosh's mum firmly. And I walked out of the kitchen.

I could hear her laughing behind me. That made me walk faster. By the time I was at the front gate I was running to get to my own house. Cute! I really *really* hated that word. I walked up our garden path, still arguing with myself as to whether or not I should shout down the phone at Mum after she'd explained about this Shelby business. I was so wrapped up in my own thoughts that my front door key was in my hand and my hand was reaching out towards the door before I realized something.

Our front door was slightly ajar.

I stared at it, my hand frozen centimetres away from the lock. I pushed it open and ran in.

'Mum? Mum, it's me! MUM!'

I dashed into the living room and stopped abruptly. It was as if I'd been kicked in the stomach by a mule. There was no sound but a strange thud-thudding in my ears as I stared around. Then I realized what that strange noise was. It was my blood, roaring like thunder through my body. The living room was in chaos.

We'd been burgled.

The VCR was gone, the telly lay on its side

and the whole room had been trashed. The sofa and armchair cushions were littered over the floor. All our CDs and tapes and videos were strewn across the carpet like a whirlwind had entered the room. The bookcase had been tipped over and all the books lay in haphazard heaps beneath it. Like a zombie I wandered from the room.

My throat felt as if it was being strangled from the inside out and my eyes began to burn with stinging tears which I couldn't stop running down my cheeks. The kitchen looked relatively untouched although the fridge door was wide open and the fridge motor was whirring loudly in protest.

So much for waking up and feeling it was going to be a brilliant day, I thought bitterly.

We'd been burgled. When had it happened? When had they arrived? How had the thieves known that the house was empty? Why now? Why us? I felt sick. I wiped the back of my hand across my eyes but I couldn't stop my eyes from leaking – which made me feel worse. I hadn't cried when the police had arrived saying they wanted to arrest Mum, so why cry now?

I went out into the hall and looked up the stairs. What was waiting for me up there? Had they taken the mini hi-fi Mum bought me for my last birthday? But then I remembered the most important thing of all – Mum's computer . . . I didn't so much run as leap up the stairs.

Please don't let them have taken it – please . . .

I raced into the back bedroom. It was still there. I couldn't believe it. I would've thought Mum's computer was the first thing the thieves would've taken. It had definitely been moved – the monitor was on the floor, the processor was by the door with the printer and scanner sitting on top of it. It was as if the thieves had planned to take it but they'd been interrupted before they could get very far. All the cables and wires were disconnected but *it was still there*. I lifted up the printer to put it back on the table before it occurred to me that maybe I shouldn't. I didn't want to smudge the burglars' fingerprints. I put it back down on the monitor and went to see what exactly had been taken from the other rooms.

The bathroom was untouched. In my bedroom, all my things had been moved, my books and CDs were scattered across the floor, they'd even tipped my mattress off the base of my bed, but nothing seemed to be missing and it was the same story in Mum's bedroom – as far as I could see. Was our video recorder really the only thing that had been taken? The thieves had to have been interrupted, there was no other explanation.

But then, they seemed to have had time to turn the place into a tip . . . I didn't understand why they hadn't taken lots of portable things – like my mini hi-fi, or the hi-fi downstairs or the portable TV in Mum's bedroom. OK, so Mum's computer with all its gear was too heavy and cumbersome to shift but there was plenty of other stuff in the house worth taking. Not that I was complaining or anything, but it was bizarre. I ran downstairs to phone the police. It was only when I got to the phone that I remembered something else. *Mum.* I looked down at my watch. Nine-twenty-five. Mum said she'd phone at nine-fifteen and she was a stickler for things like that.

Was she all right? Had something happened?

I closed my eyes and clenched my fists against all the feelings threatening to overwhelm me. It was as if I was at the bottom of the sea desperately swimming upwards, but no matter how hard I kicked I never got to the surface. What next, for goodness' sake? *What next?*

'Emergency. Which service do you require?'

'We've been burgled,' I told the anonymous voice at the other end of the phone.

'I'll connect you through to the police,' the woman's voice told me.

Moments later I was explaining what had happened to the policeman who answered.

'Stay put, try not to touch anything and we'll send someone around straight away,' he said.

I put the phone down, hoping that Mum hadn't tried to contact me when I was on the phone to the police. I glared at the phone, willing her to ring me, missing her more than I'd ever thought possible.

'It wouldn't have killed you to wait for . . .' Nosh's voice trailed off as he looked at me. 'What's the matter?'

'We've been burgled.'

'You're kidding.'

I didn't even bother to answer. I just looked at him. I mean, did it look like I was kidding? Being burgled wasn't exactly something I'd joke about.

'What did they take?' Nosh asked, when he saw that I was serious.

'Just the video recorder as far as I can see.'

Nosh walked into the living room. He gave a long, low whistle when he saw what had happened in there. It was that more than anything else that finally convinced me that I wasn't dreaming. I sat on the second to last stair, the phone cradled in my lap, and waited.

The police arrived in about ten minutes. Mum didn't phone. And within two minutes of the two policemen arriving, Nosh's whole family was in my house.

'What's going on?'

'Burgled!'

'Why didn't you come and tell us, Nosh?'

'Elliot, I'm so sorry.'

And on and on Nosh's parents went. Only Halle said anything of any use. She took a look around the living room, turned to me and said vehemently, 'What a bunch of scumbags! I hope whoever took your VCR has the thing blow up on them – taking their favourite video with it!'

She smiled at me then and I couldn't help but smile back.

As for the police, when they arrived, we went into the living room. They let me put the sofa cushions back where they should be and we all sat down. They asked me lots of questions about where my parents were and when was the last time I'd heard from my mum, but precious little about the burglary. There were two of them, although only one asked me any questions. Then the fingerprint officer arrived. She had this gloomy, forlorn look on her face that looked like it was permanently painted on. She disappeared off somewhere muttering something about her raging indigestion. She came back less than five minutes later, shaking her head.

'It looks like a professional job. They came in through the back via the kitchen window. There were two of them but they were both wearing gloves.'

'Not much chance of catching them, then,' the head policeman said glumly.

Yep! If today was going to be a brilliant day, I should definitely get back into bed and wait for tomorrow, I decided.

'You're not staying here by yourself, are you?' asked the glum policeman.

I shook my head. 'I'm staying with Nosh's family next door until my mum gets back,' I replied.

He wrote something in his book.

'Well,' he said, standing up, 'I can give you a crime number which your mum will have to use to claim on her insurance.'

'Is that it, then?' I asked, surprised.

'The thieves are long gone now, but we'll see what we can do.'

Was I impressed? Not much! But what could I do? Missing Mum more than ever, I began to straighten up the room.

'I'm meeting Julian in an hour. We're joining the ANTIDOTE protest march against Shelby's later this afternoon but I'll stay and help you tidy up until then,' Halle told me.

'I'll stay for a while too,' said Nosh's dad. 'I can't let you clear up this mess by yourself.'

'I'll see you later, Elliot,' Nosh told me.

'Nosh!' His dad and mum spoke in shocked unison.

'I'm only joking.' Nosh grinned. 'I wouldn't run out now, would I?'

'Hhmm! I wouldn't put it past you,' said his mum.

'I'll start on the upstairs,' I said quietly.

I could feel my eyes stinging again and I didn't fancy embarrassing myself in front of my neighbours. I trudged up the stairs, thankful that no-one tried to stop me.

'D'you want some help?' Nosh called after me.

I turned back to him. 'Yeah, OK,' I said at last.

Nosh followed me into Mum's computer room.

'You can help me get this lot sorted out,' I said when at last I could trust myself not to blub.

We put the processor under the table and moved the PC screen onto the table next to the printer. Nosh sorted out the cables strewn across the floor, whilst I tried to figure out what I needed to do to make Mum's PC work again. Actually it was the best thing I could do in the circumstances. I soon became so engrossed with what I was doing that it took my mind off . . . other things. Not completely, but enough for me to calm down inside. All the cables and wires were still present so Nosh and I set about connecting the whole system up again. It took a while but at last we were plugged in and ready to give it a go. I turned on the speakers and the screen before turning on the processor. Text immediately came up on the monitor.

'Yes! It still works,' I grinned at Nosh.

'Of course it does,' Nosh grinned back. 'We did it!'

But I'd spoken too soon. About two seconds after we got the initial message about booting up the computer, the system crashed. My smile faded. I pressed the <RESET> button on the processor to try again. The same thing happened. I dug Mum's boot-up disk out of the pen-tray of the table and inserted that in the floppy disk drive. This time the computer booted up properly, using the floppy disk – but it might as well not have bothered. There was absolutely nothing on Mum's computer. The directories, the files – they'd all gone. The hard disk was empty. It wasn't that the hard disk was corrupt and wouldn't allow us to read any files, there just wasn't anything there. Nothing. And ANTIDOTE.CONFIDENTIAL – the Marcus Pardela memo that Mum had loaded – that had gone, too.

'What's going on? Where's all the stuff we were looking at yesterday?' Nosh asked me, puzzled.

I stared at the screen. 'It's all been erased. A total wipe-out.'

'I don't understand.' Nosh frowned.

'I mean, someone has deliberately wiped out every file Mum had on the system,' I said. 'Now why would a burglar – a real burglar – sit down and take the time to do that?'

8

The Protest March

'What're you saying? That the people who broke into this house weren't real burglars at all?' Nosh asked, astounded.

'Why would they take the time to sit here and wipe out every file, then not take the computer?' I asked. 'Why not take the computer, then delete all the files once they got it home or something?'

'It doesn't make any sense,' Nosh agreed.

'Nothing about this whole business does,' I said. 'I mean, how come the burglars knew the one and only night in the last year and a half when there was no-one at home? Don't you think that's a bit of a coincidence?'

'Are you sure you're not getting a bit carried away?' frowned Nosh.

'Nosh, look around. Nothing was taken – nothing except an old VCR. I reckon that was only taken to make it *look* like a burglary.'

'But what about all the mess . . . ?'

'I've been thinking about that, too. The

only explanation I can come up with is that the so-called burglars were looking for something.'

'Like what?'

I shrugged. 'I don't know. Maybe they knew about Marcus Pardela's confidential memo and wanted to get that back. Or maybe they were looking for Mum's personal organizer. That could be why she told me to take the organizer and put it somewhere safe.'

'Is that what she told you to do when she phoned you last night?' Nosh asked curiously.

I grimaced and bit my lip. Me and my ginormous mouth! 'Yes, but don't tell anyone else. Mum warned me not to say anything to anyone.'

'I won't tell a soul. You can count on me. But what I don't understand is why anyone would be after your mum's organizer?'

'I DON'T KNOW!' I exploded. 'Stop asking stupid questions I can't answer.'

'Well, excuse me whilst I just run after my bloomin' head.'

We both sat in silence staring at the monitor.

'Those two men we saw last night,' Nosh said suddenly. 'D'you think they were the burglars?'

The moment he said that, I instantly felt that he was right. And then I told myself off.

'It's not very likely,' I pointed out, doubtfully.

'But if you're right about this not being a real burglary then it makes sense,' Nosh insisted. 'Those two men were watching your house. They only turned away when they noticed that we were watching them.'

'That doesn't help much. We don't know who they were or where they were from and there's no way the police would buy a story like that.'

'Hhmm!' Nosh agreed reluctantly. 'I wonder why they wiped out your mum's disk?'

'Obviously because there was something on it that they didn't want Mum or anyone else to see or keep,' I replied. 'But if it was the Marcus Pardela memo, why not just delete that one file?'

'I wonder if it *was* that?' Nosh spoke more to himself than to me.

'This is so frustrating.' I slammed my hand against the table which was stupid because I came off worse! 'If I could just begin to make sense of one thing, then maybe everything else would fall into place but at the moment I feel like I'm rushing around in all directions in the dark.'

'I take it your mum didn't phone you this morning?'

I shook my head.

'Should we go on the ANTIDOTE protest march?' Nosh asked. 'It seems to me that that's the most likely place now to find some answers.'

'OK,' I agreed. 'I don't see that we've got much to lose. We could go with Halle and her boyfriend . . .'

'You must be nuts!' Nosh told me indignantly. 'I'm not going anywhere with those two.'

'But . . .'

'No way,' said Nosh.

And that was the end of that. After one last look at the PC screen, I turned off the processor.

We spent the rest of the morning trying to return the house to normal. Nosh's dad phoned a glazier who promised to arrive within the hour to fix the glass in the kitchen window.

'I don't have enough money to pay him,' I told Nosh's dad reluctantly.

'Don't worry about it. I'll pay and I'll sort it out with your mum later,' Nosh's dad insisted.

He was being so nice, I felt guilty for all the begrudging thoughts I'd had about him the night before. When it got to half-twelve, most of the house was back to normal.

'Mum, Dad, d'you mind if Elliot and I go out? I think Elliot needs to get away from here for a while,' Nosh said.

'Where will you go?' Nosh's mum asked.

'We thought we could go to the pictures or something,' Nosh told them.

I kept my mouth shut, wondering why he didn't just tell them that we wanted to join the ANTIDOTE march.

'D'you need any money?'

'No, we've got enough,' Nosh replied.

'OK, just be back home by five,' Nosh's mum said at last.

'Thanks, Mum,' Nosh smiled.

'And don't worry, Elliot, we'll keep a close eye on the house,' Nosh's dad added.

'Thanks,' I said gratefully.

As we left the house, I asked, 'What was that all about?'

'Mum and Dad would never have let us go on the ANTIDOTE march,' Nosh explained. 'They cut up rough when Halle said she wanted to go, and in the end they only agreed because scabby Julian said he was going with her.'

'Why're they so against the idea?'

Nosh lowered his voice. 'They reckon with any march that big, you're bound to get some yobbos coming along just to make trouble.'

'Then maybe we should hook up with Halle

and her boyfriend, just to be on the safe side?' I suggested.

'No. Besides, there's nothing Halle would like better than to run home and tell Mum and Dad that we went on the march.'

I shrugged. I wasn't going to argue but I thought Nosh was making a mistake.

An hour later we caught up with the ANTI-DOTE march when they were less than a kilometre away from Shelby and Pardela Pharmaceuticals. The crowd of people marching in the protest seemed to be at least two kilometres long in itself. Four abreast, people were holding banners and placards railing against Shelby's. The police who walked alongside were few and far between. They obviously didn't expect that much trouble. And the faces of the officers I could see looked more cheesed off at having to be there in the first place, than worried or alert. We had a scout about but we could see no sign of Halle and Julian. Nosh was more relieved than anything else.

'Let's walk a bit faster to the front of the march,' I suggested. 'That ANTIDOTE woman I saw on the telly – what was her name? – Sarah Irving, she's bound to be at the front somewhere.'

'D'you know any of the other heads of ANTIDOTE?' Nosh asked.

'Only their names. Let's see . . . there was Somebody Macmillan – I think his name was Ian. Rohan Adjava – I remember his name 'cause it reminded me of coffee – and my uncle, of course.'

'Never mind. If any of them are here, we'll find them. Let's search for Sarah Irving,' said Nosh.

We started to make our way through the crowd.

'What happens when we find her?' I asked, turning my head every which way in the hope of spying her. 'I mean, she might be the Shelby agent.'

'We'll just have to be very careful,' Nosh shrugged.

Which was a big help! Nosh spotted them first – Halle and her boyfriend. They were halfway down the march, each holding one end of a banner.

'Don't let them see us,' Nosh hissed.

We bent low and skirted the outside of the march, making a run for it once we were past them.

'Phew! That was close,' said Nosh when we straightened up.

To be honest, I still didn't see what all that cloak and dagger stuff was about, but I didn't say anything. After all, Halle was Nosh's sister, not mine.

The march reached the Shelby building before we got anywhere near the front.

'I hope we haven't fought our way to the front for nothing,' I frowned, still looking around.

'Look!' Nosh pointed to the huge, wrought-iron Shelby gates.

A woman and a man, their arms laden down with masses of paper, were arguing with the eight security guards at the gates. Nosh and I scooted past the two policemen at the front of the march who were trying to hold everyone back, and ran up to the gates.

'I told you, all we want to do is deliver this petition,' the woman said angrily.

'And I told you that you can deliver it to me,' said the head security guard who looked just like a Nazi guard out of one of those old-time war films.

'I want to make sure it gets to Marcus Pardela,' said the woman.

'It will,' the guard insisted.

'We're not moving until I deliver this to the main reception.'

'That's up to you,' said the guard. 'I get paid whether you're here or not. No skin off my nose!'

The man and woman moved back a bit to talk to each other in private. They didn't notice Nosh and me listening.

'Sarah, we're wasting our time. They're never going to let us pass,' said the man.

'Ian, I'm not leaving without handing in our petition to the receptionist or someone on the inside of the building. If we give it to that security guard, it'll get filed under "B"!'

'He won't put it in the bin. Not if we tell him that we'll be insisting that Marcus Pardela answer some of the points raised in the document attached to the petition. If we say that then he'll have no choice but to hand it over.'

'You think so?' Sarah asked doubtfully.

'It's worth a try,' Ian replied.

'Are you Ian Macmillan?' I asked the man.

He gave a start, then frowned down at me. 'Who wants to know?'

'Robert Gaines is my uncle,' I explained.

His eyes widened. Immediately the expression on his face changed.

'You must be Elliot,' he smiled. 'I'm sorry to be so surly but it's been a long morning and it looks like being a longer afternoon.'

'Hi, I'm Sarah Irving.' The woman held out her hand which I shook. 'We're really sorry about your mum and uncle. We're doing everything we can to get the situation resolved. Our lawyers are working on it right now.'

'Have you seen my uncle? Is he all right?' I asked, eagerly.

A look passed between Sarah and Ian.

'No, we haven't seen him. Not yet,' Sarah replied. 'We thought we'd go to see him this afternoon or maybe tomorrow.'

'Where is he?' I asked.

'He's being held at the local police station until he appears before magistrates on Monday morning,' said Sarah.

I was puzzled. I was sure the police had said Uncle Robert would appear before magistrates today, not on Monday. I'd obviously got it wrong.

'Has Mum been in touch with you?' I asked, after a brief pause.

'No, not yet.' The two grown-ups exchanged another glance. This time Ian spoke. 'We were hoping she'd get in touch with us. To be honest, we're not quite sure where she fits in to all of this. So she hasn't been in touch with you either?'

I shook my head, saying the words, 'Not today . . .' in my mind, so that it wasn't a complete lie.

'The police say they have a video tape that shows Uncle Robert and Mum breaking into Shelby's . . .' I began.

'Yeah, we were sent a copy of the video tape, too – no doubt to rub our noses in it,' said Ian with disgust.

'Did . . . did your Uncle Robert tell you

what he and your mother intended to do?'
Sarah asked.

'You make it sound like they both did it,' I
snapped out at her.

'But we've seen the video tape . . .' Sarah
began.

'I don't care. Mum said that tape is a
fake . . .'

It was only when I felt Nosh's warning hand
on my arm that I realized what I'd said.

'I mean, Mum would say it was a fake if she
was here,' I finished weakly.

From the look on Ian's and Sarah's faces, it
was obvious I hadn't fooled them for a
second.

'Is there any chance of my seeing the tape,
please?' I asked.

'We are rather busy at the moment . . .'
Sarah frowned.

'Please,' I pleaded. 'I haven't seen my mum
since late Friday afternoon and my uncle's
been arrested. I just want to look at it to see
what the evidence is against them. It would
help me to try and make sense of what's going
on. *Please*.'

Ian frowned at me then turned to Sarah.
'Look, Sarah, you can deliver this petition
with Jack and some of the others. I'll take
Elliot to the office. It's only a five minute walk
from here and it won't take long.'

'But Ian, you're needed here,' Sarah argued.

'Sarah, you're in charge and we both know you can handle things perfectly well without me,' Ian smiled. 'Besides, Robert has helped me out of a few sticky situations in the past. The least I can do is help his nephew now.'

Sarah didn't look the least bit happy but I didn't care. Scrutinizing her through narrowed eyes, I reckoned she was mean enough to be the Shelby agent. I turned to smile at Nosh. We were going to see the video. That was a step in the right direction at any rate. At last I was making progress. Just the thought that I was *doing* something felt good.

Nosh and I made our way through the front of the crowd, followed by Ian. This old biddy arrived from nowhere and tried to push past me. I'm surprised she didn't just lift me up and move me bodily out of her way. She was wearing a floppy hat held on by a faded scarf which hid most of her face, and slung over her arm was a grubby raincoat.

'Excuse me all over the place!' I said indignantly.

But she'd already trodden on my left foot, elbowed me in the ribs and gone forward to assault someone else. I turned to scowl at her. My mum wouldn't let me get away with anything like that, but many grown-ups don't even have two manners in their bodies to keep each other company! That was one of my mum's truer sayings. And she'd got it from my nan!

'She bashed into me, too,' Nosh sniffed. 'Some people!'

'Let's duck down one of these side roads. It'll be faster,' Ian suggested.

As soon as we'd turned off the main street it was as if the decrease volume button on a TV remote had been pressed. The increasing peace gave me a chance to think about the video we were about to see.

'D-Did Uncle Robert try to break into Shelby's Pharmaceuticals for ANTIDOTE?' I didn't want to, but I had to ask. I had to *know*.

Ian gave me a considering look.

'The tape seems to indicate that he did . . .' he began.

'But did you *ask* him to?' I questioned urgently.

Ian looked up and down the street before turning back to me.

'Elliot, sometimes . . . sometimes you have to do the wrong thing for the right reason,' Ian said softly.

So I had my answer.

'Mum always says "two wrongs don't make a right",' I told him.

'Does she also say "the ends justifies the means"?'

'Not that I remember,' I replied.

'I'm sure in this case, she would,' Ian told me.

'The only end result I can see is that my uncle is locked up and my mum is missing,' I said coldly.

'Yes, that is rather unfortunate . . .' Ian muttered.

I don't think I was meant to hear that bit, but I did. *Unfortunate!* Not winning the national lottery was *unfortunate*. What had happened to my family was disastrous! It's amazing how fast you can go off some people. As I glowered up at Ian, I found myself liking Sarah Irving more and more.

You did it! You're the Shelby agent! I decided as I regarded Ian.

I clamped my lips together tightly, trying my best not to rant at him but my blood was boiling.

'So who has the original of the tape you're going to show us?' Nosh leapt in just as I opened my mouth – which was probably just as well.

'The police, I assume,' said Ian.

'And there's no doubt at all about it being Elliot's uncle?' Nosh questioned.

'None. You'll see for yourself in a minute,' Ian told us.

We walked on in silence with Ian leading the way, each of us deep in thought. Five minutes later, we entered an unmarked door between a stationery shop and an Italian restaurant and headed up some stairs. At the top of the stairs, there was a huge open-plan office with tables and PCs and a fax machine and a large photo-copier scattered about. A lean man and a tiny woman sat at one of the desks both peering at a computer screen. The rest of the place was deserted.

'Hi, Rohan. Still working?' Ian called over to the man.

'Yep! I still can't figure out why our network went down yesterday,' Rohan sighed.

'You'll work it out,' Ian said confidently.

'Hopefully before I die of starvation!' the woman next to Rohan complained.

'I'll take you for lunch as soon as I get it working,' Rohan promised.

'Yeah, right.' She sat back in her seat looking distinctly unimpressed.

Ian led the way across the other end of the office to a desk which had more clutter on it than any of the others.

'Grab two chairs. I'll just set this up,' he told us.

Nosh and I picked up two chairs and placed

them on either side of Ian as he powered up his PC. He had a system like my mum's, only not quite as good. Once again, I found myself wondering just why Mum needed our extensive, expensive system. Ian unlocked his desk and took out an unlabelled video tape. He pushed the video tape into the VCR under his table and then started the necessary program on his PC to play it. I pulled my chair in closer. The video started playing in a framed box in the middle of the screen. Ian pressed a couple of buttons and the video picture filled the screen. I recognized the scene immediately.

It was twilight, not quite dark yet. In spite of the fading light, the Shelby building was brightly illuminated by the spotlights dotted all around the immediate grounds and the building itself. There was no sound. All we could hear was the inaudible arguing of Rohan and his girlfriend at the other end of the open plan. Then, without warning, two figures ran into view on the video tape, their backs to the closed-circuit TV camera which was recording. They skirted the side of the building before turning out of sight of the camera. Immediately another closed-circuit camera took over, filming the two people as they made their cautious way around the back of the building. One of the figures took out something which looked like a credit card from a small backpack he or she was carrying and started to fiddle with the electronic keypad beside the double doors. It was hard to make out who the figures were. So far we'd only seen their backs, or the briefest side view. Within moments, however, the double doors opened and they were inside. It was only then that the interior camera – and us – got a good look at their faces. They began to make their way up the stairs, then one of them stopped and pointed to the camera directly ahead and above them – and there the image on the screen froze. It was Mum and Uncle Robert.

And Mum was the one who pointed at the camera.

9

The Present

I shook my head in disbelief. I couldn't believe it. I was seeing it and still I couldn't believe it.

'That's where the tape finishes,' Ian said.

'What software are you using to play back this video?' I asked stonily.

Ian told me. It was the same software package my mum used.

'Can I try something?' I asked Ian.

'I don't think that would be wise . . .' he began doubtfully. 'This is the only copy of the tape we have.'

'I'll be careful, I promise. I know what I'm doing.'

Reluctantly he swapped seats with me. From the keyboard I rewound the video tape and played it again. I zoomed into the image of the backs of the two people as they skirted the side of the building. The image was indistinct, a bit fuzzy. I tried to enhance the image but it didn't make any difference. It didn't make it any clearer. I zoomed out again. The two figures then turned the corner and the video continued seamlessly. There was barely a gap or a jump in the video tape. I played the rest of the tape in slow motion until the two figures got inside. Then I replayed the tape in the slowest motion possible. And still I could see nothing wrong. But Mum said the tape was a fake and I believed her. Somehow, someone had doctored the tape and I had to find out how. I sat back and frowned.

'What d'you think?' Nosh said.

I shook my head. 'I'm not sure. I think I'll play the whole thing frame by frame.'

'What does that mean?' Nosh asked me.

'When you make a film or a video, you have to make sure that when people walk and run or whatever, they move like real people and not jerkily like puppets. The way it works is that film or video cameras capture at least twenty-four images a second. That way, when the whole thing is played back at normal speed, the film makes everything look smooth and like ordinary movements. Playing something frame by frame means going through every single image individually, then you can see every little gesture or movement broken down. At least that's how Mum explained it to me. Is that right, Ian?'

Ian shrugged and looked perplexed. 'If she said so.'

I rewound the tape until it was back at the beginning again. Then I played each frame individually rather than letting the tape run normally. Beside me I could hear Ian huffing with impatience but I wasn't going to let that stop me. This was my mum and uncle, not his. And then I found something.

'Nosh, look at that,' I said, excitedly.

'At what?'

I used the left arrow key on the keypad to go back a few frames, then pressed the space bar to go forward slowly.

'Did you see that?' I asked.

'See what?' Nosh asked.

I played it again. From the look on Nosh's face – and Ian's – neither of them was the wiser.

'Watch what happens when the two figures go round the corner. Look at their heads,' I instructed.

And I played the tape in the slowest motion for a third time. Nosh leaned closer, his frown deepening.

'There was something there – just for a second, and then it disappeared,' he said, puzzled.

'You saw it too,' I beamed at him. 'I knew I wasn't imagining things.'

'What? I didn't see anything,' Ian complained.

I went back to the one frame that was peculiar and froze the image. 'Look at the heads.'

'They're darker and look slightly different. So what?' Ian shrugged.

'Their heads are darker because the two people in the video at this point are wearing hoods or masks of some kind,' I said. 'Look closely and you can see. If you run the tape at normal speed it's just one frame of twenty-four which flash by in less than a second. That's why you miss it. But if you run the tape frame by frame then you can see it, but only in this one frame.'

'Play it again,' Ian ordered. His nose was practically against the screen now.

I did as he said and played the tape again.

'Can't you zoom in any closer than that?' he asked.

'I should be able to with this software but every time I try, the video quality gets worse,' I explained. 'I think this tape has definitely been doctored, just to make sure that no-one can zoom in close and see what's really going on.'

Ian pushed my hands off the keyboard and replayed the bit where the two people came round the corner for himself.

'D'you know, I think you're right about that frame of the video,' he said at last. 'I think they *are* wearing something over their heads, and then in the next frame the backs of their heads are lighter again. The masks or hoods or whatever have been removed.'

'Can you alter video tapes like that?' Nosh asked me, surprised.

I raised my eyebrows. 'Are you kidding? With a computer and the right software I could put the president of America's head on Mum's body and vice versa. If you know what you're doing, it's a doddle.'

'But one measly frame isn't much proof that your mum and your uncle have been set up,' Nosh said.

'It's a start,' I argued. 'And if the police have the same tape then they'll have the same evidence as us.'

'Then how come they haven't found the same thing as us?' Nosh asked.

'How do we know they haven't?' Ian suggested.

'I'd be surprised if they're even looking,' I pointed out. 'After all, they think they have a proper tape showing real evidence. They'd just run it at normal speed. Why would they run it a frame at a time? It takes ages that way and as far as they're concerned, there's no point.'

'How did you know there was something wrong with the tape?' Ian asked.

I opened my mouth to answer, only to close and open and close it again like a drowning fish. It was only when he asked the question that I remembered who he was – and who he might be. He worked for ANTIDOTE. And while he might not be the mole secretly working for Shelby's, he might inadvertently blab and say something to the real agent. I reckoned I'd said enough, if not far too much already.

'I just know my mum didn't try to break into that place,' I replied, trying to make my voice sound natural. 'So if she didn't, then this video tape must be a fake.'

'And you know all about computers?' Ian questioned.

'Not all about them,' I denied.

'But more than most,' Nosh grinned.

I cast him a warning look. He got the message straight away.

'You're a clever boy, aren't you?' said Ian, making it sound like I had virulent, contagious flu or something. 'Your uncle is always talking about how clever you are.'

'Is he?' What was I meant to say to that? Ian didn't even say it like it was a compliment – more like an insult. But as he'd brought the subject up, I decided to chance my arm.

'D'you mind if I see where my uncle works?'

'Pardon?'

'His desk? Can I see where he works?' I repeated.

Ian frowned. 'If you want. But I warn you now, the police took away most of his personal belongings early this morning. It happened before any of us arrived. A volunteer let them take away your uncle's stuff without a warrant.' His tone of voice showed only too clearly what he thought of the volunteer's actions. It didn't take a genius to imagine the full and frank discussion that followed when Ian had arrived at work and found out what had happened.

He stood up and led the way over to a cluttered desk in a corner of the open plan. I sat down in Uncle's chair and had a look around. A multimedia PC, a modem and a printer dominated most of the space on the desk. Any remaining space was filled with papers and files and folders. There was a photo of Uncle, Mum and me pinned to the wall as well as a huge, poster-sized calendar of the whole year. Red dots and gold stickers and green strips were scattered all over the calendar. I looked closer. There was a red dot over my birthday of August 30th and another one over Mum's birthday of February 8th. I didn't recognize the other red 'dotted' dates. I looked from the

PC to the calendar and wondered why Uncle Robert would bother with a calendar when there was bound to be a proper scheduler on his PC. Mum used to say that Uncle Robert was like a big kid. He had to have every new software product going – games, word processors, spreadsheets, databases, schedulers, you name it, he had it.

'Can I switch on the PC?' I asked Ian.

'Why?'

'Uncle Robert wrote a game for me and I'm finding it difficult to get started with it. I thought there might be some clues on his machine.' I said the first thing that came into my head. Then I realized something else. I hadn't actually had the chance to play with Uncle's game yet. With everything that had been going on recently, it had completely slipped my mind.

'Go on, then. If you think it will help,' Ian said sceptically.

I switched on the PC processor. The screen and the loudspeakers came on automatically, unlike on Mum's machine where you have to switch on every peripheral individually. Within moments, there was a message on the screen:

SYSTEM DISK FAILURE: ALL DATA IS LOST. REBOOT FROM FLOPPY.

I gasped, as did Ian and Nosh. First Mum's machine. Now Uncle Robert's. That had to be more than just a coincidence.

'Those blundering police!' Ian fumed. 'Look what they've done. They were messing about on Robert's machine and now they've lost all his data.'

I looked up at Ian. Some gut instinct told me that someone had been messing about on Uncle Robert's machine, but it hadn't been the police . . .

'Ian, I think you'd better get over here,' Rohan called out from across the office.

'What is it?' Ian yelled back.

'We're on the telly,' Rohan replied.

'Good or bad?'

'Bad.'

Ian turned and practically ran across the open plan. Nosh followed him. I got up but lagged behind a bit. After a quick glance around, I opened up Uncle's top drawer. Papers and more papers. The second drawer was even worse. Closing the drawers, I pulled open the pen tray at the top of the desk. Right at the back of the pen tray, in the deepest recess, was a tape cartridge. There was no way to see it if you didn't pull the pen tray right out as far as it would go. I instantly knew what was on the tape cartridge. It was a back-up of all the data that had been on Uncle's PC. The only question was, how old was the back-up? As I picked up the tape, a folded piece of paper was revealed beneath it. Putting the tape into my pocket, I then nosed at the piece of paper. It was Uncle's Internet address and password. I put that in my pocket too before closing the pen tray.

Thank goodness Uncle Robert was so PC conscientious. He was always reminding me never to do anything on a PC without taking a back-up afterwards. I knew he had to have a back-up tape somewhere and I remembered him saying he kept one in his desk as well as another one at home. I turned off the PC and followed Nosh and Ian to the other end of the open plan.

'What were you doing over there?' Ian's eyes narrowed as he watched me.

'Turning off the PC,' I answered. I turned away, hoping I didn't look too guilty.

Rohan was pointing a remote control up at the TV mounted against one wall. The TV volume began to increase. I recognized the face of the man on the telly instantly. It was Marcus Pardela.

'. . . *Just the sort of underhand tactic that a group like ANTIDOTE would use,*' Marcus said to the interviewer who stood before him. '*One of their operatives, a man called Robert*

Gaines, is already in police custody for trying to break into our main industrial plant, and I understand it's only a matter of time before his accomplice, his sister-in-law Lisa Gaines, is picked up by the police as well. And now on top of all that, we have a few more misguided ANTIDOTE individuals actually trying to set fire to our plant today after their so-called protest march. They profess to be animal lovers and to care for the environment and yet they think nothing of putting innocent lives at risk and . . .'

'Switch it off,' Ian ordered.

Rohan frowned at him.

'SWITCH IT OFF!' Ian said furiously.

Rohan used the remote control to comply.

'What the hell was that all about?' Ian demanded. 'What fire is he talking about?'

'Apparently, someone tried to set fire to the Shelby plant. The fire brigade had to be called out. It was a very small fire and it's under control now but you know how the press loves to distort these things,' Rohan explained.

'How did they get hold of Marcus Pardela so quickly?' Ian asked.

'He was already in the Shelby building apparently,' said Rohan.

'It wouldn't surprise me if that . . .' Ian glanced at me and Nosh, and obviously changed what he'd been about to say, 'if that *man* had started the fire himself, just to discredit us,' Ian stormed.

'He'd never do his own dirty work,' Rohan sniffed. 'Someone in the crowd on our march obviously did his dirty work for him.'

I was very aware of Nosh by now as we made a concerted effort *not* to look at each other. That scenario was exactly what was going on in the ANTIDOTE office too. And maybe one of the two men before us already knew that. I placed my hands on my burning cheeks, trying – and failing – not to feel embarrassed because my mum's name had been mentioned on the telly. Feeling guilty, I stuffed my hands deep into my pockets. I tried to decide what my next move should be. I'd met the leaders of ANTIDOTE, I'd seen the video tape. Now what? Ian and Rohan continued to rant about Marcus Pardela.

'Nosh, maybe we should leave . . .' I began.

But then I felt something in my left pocket – something that hadn't been there before. Clasping it in my hand I took it out and stared at it. The moment I realized what it was, my fingers folded over it and I held it tight.

'What's the matter?' Nosh asked me.

Ian and Rohan stopped their discussion to look at me curiously.

'Er . . . I've just remembered, we're meant to be somewhere else. Come on, Nosh.' I grabbed Nosh by the arm and pulled him out of the office. It was only when we got to the bottom of the stairs that I took the item out of my pocket. It lay on my palm, glistening in the half light of the stairwell.

'What is it?' Nosh whispered.

'It's my mum's wedding ring,' I replied.

'What're you doing with that?' asked Nosh. 'You didn't tell me you had that.'

'I didn't have it – at least, I didn't have it this morning,' I said. 'Someone's left me a present.'

'I don't understand.'

'This ring wasn't in my pocket this morning,' I persisted.

'Then where did it come from?' asked Nosh.

'That's just what I want . . .' I heard a noise coming from the landing above and quickly raised my head. Someone above us ducked out of sight before I could see who it was.

10

I'm A Friend

'Come on, Nosh. We have work to do.' I pulled Nosh out into the street after me.

'Elliot, will you please tell me what's going on?' Nosh said, exasperated.

'Someone's put this ring in my pocket.'

'When?'

'Some time between the march and me finding it just now,' I said.

'Who?'

I dug deeper into my pocket, hoping to find some clue. There was a tiny scrap of folded paper, so small I could've easily missed it if I hadn't been deliberately searching my pockets.

'What does it say?' Nosh asked breathlessly.

'21:15hrs – phone.'

'Is that from your mum?'

'It must be. I think it means she's going to phone me tonight instead . . .'

'But when did she get that note to you?'

Nosh queried. 'I know! It must've been on the march.'

'That'd be my guess,' I said thoughtfully. I was still trying to figure out exactly when, though. Then I got it! 'That old woman on the march, remember? The one who bumped into me? She must be the one who put the note in my pocket. That must've been *Mum*.'

Nosh frowned sceptically. 'Nah! It couldn't have been. You'd have recognized your own mum.'

'But I wasn't expecting to see her. And I never did get a very good look at the woman who barged into me. She was wearing a floppy hat and a scarf that covered most of her face.'

'But even so . . .'

After a moment's pause, I sighed. 'Yeah, maybe you're right. I'm just clutching at straws,' I said, wondering if I'd caught Nosh's disease of too much imagination. 'Maybe it was Mum and maybe it wasn't. I just wish I knew for certain.'

I desperately tried to remember the face of the woman who'd barged me, but all I could recall was the woman's back, stalking away from me. And besides, why all the cloak-and-dagger stuff if it was Mum? She wouldn't do that. She'd come up to me and tell me what was going on – wouldn't she? I still couldn't make head nor tail of what was going on.

Thank goodness for the school holidays. I don't think I could've gone to school and tried to carry on as if nothing was happening and everything was as normal. I felt like I was in a computer game with lasers and rockets and missiles firing at me from all directions so that I didn't know which way to turn to get away from them. I needed to sit down alone, in peace and quiet, and just consider what to do next. At the moment I was rushing around like a headless chicken. Lots of things had happened – and were still happening – but I wasn't giving myself enough time to sort through them or work them out. It was a question of stepping back and taking it more slowly.

Someone at ANTIDOTE had been listening when I showed Nosh Mum's wedding ring – only I didn't know who.

Think, Elliot. Think! What should I do next?

Mum had warned me off going to Uncle Robert's house but really, what choice did I have? The police said he'd be released on bail soon. Maybe he was at home already? I glanced down at my watch. Uncle Robert lived quite a distance away. If I went to see him, I'd never be back at Nosh's house by the time his mum had specified. I gritted my teeth. That couldn't be helped. I didn't want to go against Nosh's mum's wishes, but what choice did I have?

I looked around.

'What're you looking for?' Nosh queried.

'A phone box. I thought I'd phone my uncle and see if he's at home yet.'

'And if he is?'

The look on my face gave him his answer.

'Elliot, you can't go to see your uncle now. He lives miles away,' Nosh protested.

'You don't have to come.' I shook my head. 'I don't want to get you into trouble, so you'd better go home now.'

'No way.'

'Suit yourself. Just don't tell your mum and dad I dragged you with me,' I told him, ungraciously.

We walked back up to the main road, and even then it took a good few minutes to find a phone box that took ordinary money and not phone cards. I phoned my uncle, not really expecting much. To my surprise, the phone was picked up within three rings.

'Hello?' said a man's wary voice.

But it wasn't my uncle . . .

'Can I speak to Uncle Robert, please?'

There was a long pause.

'He's not here,' the voice replied gruffly.

'When will he be back?'

'I don't know.'

'Who am I speaking to?' I'd barely got the words out before the phone went dead. I made up my mind in a moment. 'Nosh, I'm going to my uncle's house.'

'Why? From the sound of it, he's not even in.'

'But *someone* is. And besides, Uncle Robert might return home at any minute.'

'Elliot, I know you're worried about your family and you want to feel you're doing something, but rushing around like a drunken fly won't get you very far.'

'You go home. I'll see you later,' I said stubbornly.

Nosh sighed. 'I'm coming with you – and don't bother arguing.'

I didn't. Truth to tell, I didn't want to argue with him. I was glad of the company.

One tube ride, a bus journey and a ten minute walk later, we were outside Uncle Robert's house. I rang the doorbell for the umpty-umpth time but there was no answer.

'It's OK. I'm not going to say I told you so!' Nosh folded his arms across his chest.

I scowled at him and tried the doorbell one more time for good measure. Nothing.

'Well, someone was here an hour ago,' I said.

I bent down to peer through the letterbox. Had I really come all this way for nothing?

The hall looked exactly the way I remembered it. There were a couple of unopened letters on the hall table next to the phone but that was it.

'Elliot, don't look now but I think we've got company,' Nosh whispered.

'Where?' I straightened up immediately, my head turning every which way like some kind of nodding dog.

'Elliot! I said *don't* look!' Nosh glared. 'Very subtle – I don't think.'

'Sorry!' I said and immediately kept my head still.

But I'd seen them. Two men across the street. Was it the same two men who'd been across the street from our house the night we'd been burgled? I couldn't tell, but they looked very . . . shall we say, similar. One of them had close-cropped hair, the other one was thinning on top but had a short ponytail. Out of the corner of my eye, I could see the two men talking to each other with a kind of studied nonchalance that I didn't believe for a second.

'What should we do?' Nosh asked.

I took a last look at my uncle's house which was swathed in darkness before answering Nosh's question. 'Let's go home.'

'Thank goodness for that.' Nosh breathed a sigh of relief.

'Don't look at those men. Pretend we haven't seen them,' I suggested.

'You don't have to tell me that,' Nosh said indignantly. 'I'm not the one who practically ran over to them and asked to see their driver's licences!'

'I wasn't that bad, was I?' I protested.

'You were worse,' Nosh told me.

We set off down the road towards the bus stop.

'What're they doing?' I asked, dying to turn around.

'When I sprout eyes at the back of my head, I'll tell you,' said Nosh.

Sometimes he can be a sarcastic ratbag! But this time I knew that most of it stemmed from being afraid. And he wasn't the only one. We were both a long way from home. I bent down and pretended to re-tie the shoelaces of my trainers. The two men were on the opposite side of the street but they were almost level with us. When I stopped, they stopped and started talking to each other again. I straightened up and Nosh and I carried on walking.

'They're following us,' I whispered to Nosh.

'Are you sure?'

'Well, when we stopped, they stopped,' I informed him. 'And they've both started walking in the same direction as us now.'

'What're we going to do?' Nosh asked, an anxious edge to his voice. 'Make a run for it?'

'Why? We haven't done anything!' I frowned.

'What's that got to do with the price of corned beef?' Nosh said, exasperated.

And he had a point.

'All right then, after three. One . . . two . . .'

I never made it to three.

A hand appeared from nowhere to grip my shoulder. Each finger dug into me like a steak knife. I was turned around and then the hand immediately let go. It was the guy with the pony-tail. If he hadn't let me go, I would've fought like a cornered rat. From the tense, wild look on Nosh's face, he was going to do that anyway! But when the man released me, the surprise held me still.

'Are you Elliot – Robert Gaines' nephew?' the man smiled at me. 'I saw you ringing his doorbell.'

I glanced across the street. The man's friend was crossing the road now. I took a cautious step backwards.

'I'm a friend of your uncle's,' the man continued. He held out his hand. 'My name is Allen.'

I kept my eyes on his face, ignoring his hand.

'Your uncle was released on bail this morning. He's very worried about you.' The man with the pony-tail glanced at his friend who had now joined us before turning back to me, his smile wider than ever. 'In fact, he asked me to look you up, just to make sure you're all right.'

'Where is my uncle?' I asked.

'He had to go away for a few days. I'm going to see him next week,' said the smiler. 'So can I tell him you're doing OK?'

'I'm fine,' I replied.

I didn't like the way that smile seemed to be plastered on his face. I didn't like Smiler or his friend. I took another slow step backwards, wishing Nosh would do the same. He was very close to them. Too close. Just an arm's length away.

'Have you seen your mother recently?' asked Smiler.

I shook my head.

'But you have something of hers. Something your Uncle Robert wants you to give to me,' said Smiler.

'I don't have anything . . .'

'Oh, I think you do. It's your mum's organizer. Your uncle needs it to show to the police. Apparently it has some kind of proof on it that your mum and uncle didn't break into Shelby's?'

'I don't have my mum's organizer. We were burgled. The burglars must have taken it,' I denied.

Smiler shrugged. 'That's a shame 'cause according to your uncle it's the only thing that can prove his innocence.'

'What was on it?' I asked.

'I have no idea. Your uncle just asked me to get in touch with you and ask you to hand it over to me so that I could then give it to him. He didn't go into too many details,' said Smiler.

'Why can't he get in touch with me himself?' I asked. 'What's wrong with him?'

Smiler and his friend exchanged a glance. 'There's nothing wrong with him. He's just keeping his head down for the time being – that's all.'

'How did you know I was his nephew?'

'What other boy would be knocking on his door on a Saturday afternoon?' Smiler grinned.

Yeah, right! If I had any lingering doubts, that last bit cleared them away. These two had to be the same two men who were watching our house. For all I knew, they might be the burglars as well.

'I'm sorry, we can't help you. We have to go home now,' I said. 'Come on, Nosh, or we'll miss our bus.'

'We could give you a lift if you like,' said Smiler.

A lift! With these two? Not if both my legs were broken.

'No, thank you,' I said.

'Oh, come on, Elliot. We don't bite. You're not afraid, are you?'

'No, but I'm not stupid either,' I told him. 'I'm not being funny, but I don't know you.'

I didn't want to turn my back and walk away from these two but at the same time, I didn't want to hang around them either.

'Ready, Nosh? Your mum's expecting us for dinner.'

Nosh and I walked away from the two men, our steps getting faster and faster the further we got away from them. I hardly dared breathe as I listened intently to see if they were following us.

'So you're staying with your friend, are you? I'll tell your uncle,' Smiler called out from behind me. 'He's your next-door neighbour – isn't that right?'

Goodness only knew how Nosh and I managed to keep on walking. I'd never heard anything that sounded more like a threat. It wasn't the words so much, as the way they were said, the tone of voice. It sent a chill down my back, like a single drop of icy water. The moment Nosh and I turned the corner, we looked at each other and *ran*. There was no talk, no verbal agreement, we both just did it. We ran and ran and didn't relax until we were on the bus on our way back to the tube station. I kept looking behind to see if the two men were in a car following us. Or maybe they'd got on the bus after us and we'd missed them. Maybe they were upstairs just waiting for us to get off the bus so that they could follow.

I shook my head, wondering if this was indeed what they called paranoia! Every sound, every shadow made me wince and jump. If I wasn't careful, I'd end up giving myself a heart attack or something.

And Uncle Robert? What was he doing at this precise moment? I shook my head.

'Nosh, I'm sure those two men were lying about my uncle. There's no way he'd not come and see me once he was out.'

'Are you sure?'

I didn't answer. That was the trouble. I wasn't sure of anything any more. My thoughts switched to Mum's organizer. Those two men were desperate to get their hands on it. Why? It was even more urgent that I crack Mum's password. But what to do in the meantime?

'Are you all right?' I asked Nosh quietly.

He looked straight ahead. He didn't even

acknowledge that he'd heard me. I was just about to ask the same question again when Nosh spoke. And still he didn't look at me.

'I'm scared,' he confessed.

I looked straight ahead, too. 'So am I,' I admitted.

And the worse thing was, I wasn't just scared for Mum or my uncle any more. I was scared for myself. I felt cowardly and guilty at the thought, but it was the truth.

I was scared of what I was getting myself – and Nosh – into.

11

Dangerous

'Where on earth have you two been? We've been worried sick.'

The moment the front door opened, I knew Nosh and I were in for it – and I didn't have to wait long to be proved right either. Nosh's mum looked about ready to go ballistic.

'It was all my fault, Mrs Grisham,' I said quickly. 'I went to see my Uncle Robert. I just wanted to make sure he was OK and I asked Nosh to come with me.'

Nosh took a quick glance at me but said nothing.

'Elliot, I understand that this must be a very confusing time for you and I understand your wanting to see your uncle, but I specifically asked you to be back here by five. It is now after six,' Nosh's mum said, trying to keep her voice under control.

'Yes, I know. I'm very sorry.' And I was. What more could I say? Nosh's mum and dad had been great to me and I hated causing them all this trouble. 'Maybe I should just go back next door. I'm sure Mum will be home . . .'

'Don't be silly. You can't stay in your house by yourself,' Nosh's mum immediately dismissed. 'I want the two of you to promise me that when I tell you to be home by a certain time then you'll make sure that you are.'

'We promise.'

'We promise.'

'Then we'll say no more about it,' Nosh's mum smiled. 'I've saved you both some dinner, although it's probably a dried-out mess in the oven by now.'

Nosh's mum turned and led the way to the kitchen. I looked into the living room as we passed by. Halle was sitting in an armchair, reading a magazine. She looked up at me and smiled, before returning to her magazine.

Then it hit me! Like a light bulb thrown at the back of my head! Halle was perfect! Ideal! I'd had a brilliant idea and if Halle would just go along with it, then all my problems – well, most of them – would be solved. I knew Nosh wouldn't like the idea, but tough! The only trouble was, how to convince Halle.

'You didn't have to take the blame for me,' Nosh whispered.

'Huh?'

'Telling Mum that you asked me to come

with you. We both know that wasn't true,' said Nosh.

'It doesn't matter. Besides, I didn't want to get you into any more trouble with your mum and dad,' I said.

'I can handle them,' Nosh said with disdain.

I was saved from answering by Nosh's mum producing a cottage pie out of the oven. The potato at the top was a bit dried-out and crusty but beggars couldn't be choosers – especially when it was down to us that the pie had dried out in the first place! I had the sense to keep my mouth shut. Nosh didn't!

'Didn't you make some gravy separately to go with the pie, Mum?' he complained.

What a twit! His mum was only just beginning to cool down about the two of us returning an hour later than she had told us to. With that one sentence, he managed to heat her right up again!

'Nosh, you ungrateful wretch,' she began. 'If you'd come home when I'd told you to, then the pie wouldn't need gravy or great dollops of tomato ketchup or anything else. And what's more . . .'

I kicked Nosh under the table. He looked at me ruefully and mouthed, 'Sorry!' Which was too little, too late by then.

'The pie's lovely,' I tried to placate her, but

it took a good ten minutes for Nosh's mum to calm down again. And only then because I volunteered Nosh and I to do the washing up. Which of course meant that then Nosh was mad at *me*.

'I was just trying to help,' I told him when his mum left the room. 'I can't win, can I?'

'Couldn't you have offered to do something else? I hate washing up,' Nosh grumbled.

'Quit griping. It won't take long. Besides, I've had an idea and I want to run it by you,' I told him. 'You wash and I'll dry.'

'Why not the other way around?'

''Cause it's your house,' I said. And there wasn't a lot he could say in reply!

And as I'd guessed, he didn't like my idea – at all.

'Why do we have to include her? She'll want to take over and know what we're doing every step of the way,' Nosh argued. 'And besides which, she's a girl!'

'But she can help us,' I said.

'But . . . but . . .' Nosh looked really unhappy. I almost felt sorry for him.

'If you've got any better suggestions, I'm all ears!' I told him.

I could almost see the wheels going around in Nosh's head as he desperately tried – and failed – to come up with something else.

'I suppose it might work,' he conceded at

last. 'If she doesn't bog things up and make things worse.'

'How could they be worse?' I asked.

By the time the washing up was finished and Nosh had had a chance to think over my plan, he was in a bit of a mood. I wasn't going to let that stop me. We made our way to the living room where Halle was still reading her magazine.

'You going out tonight?' Nosh asked her.

'What's it to you, you nosy bag chops?' Halle didn't even lift her head to insult her brother.

'Halle, can I ask you something?' I began, before Nosh and Halle could get into another one of their 'discussions'.

Halle raised her head and smiled. 'Of course you can.'

Nosh snorted with disgust. I ignored him.

'Do you still belong to ANTIDOTE?'

'Yes, of course. I was on their march today,' Halle said.

'Shame they weren't marching to Inverness!' Nosh muttered from beside me, but this time he had the sense to keep his remarks to himself.

'No, I mean – do you still *officially* belong to ANTIDOTE?'

'Yep! Why?'

'Would you be prepared to help me with

something? I know it's asking a bit much and I wouldn't ask you at all if I could think of some other way of doing it but I can't, and I'm desperate and . . .'

'Elliot, I have no idea what you're talking about,' Halle interrupted.

I took a deep breath to stop myself from rambling and tried to explain. 'My uncle used to work for ANTIDOTE, before . . . before all this business started.'

'Yes, I know.' Halle nodded and waited for me to continue.

'Well, he told my mum that there's something . . . not quite right going on at ANTIDOTE. I think that's why he and Mum were framed for something they didn't do,' I said. 'So I was wondering if you could volunteer to work at the ANTIDOTE offices again. It'd only be for a few hours a day – just until the holidays are over – and then maybe you could find out a bit more about what's going on.'

Halle's magazine lay forgotten on her lap. 'Exactly what did you have in mind?'

'I thought maybe if you could have a hunt around on their computers or in their filing cabinets or something, you might find out something that Mum and my uncle can use. Something that will explain all this,' I said eagerly.

Halle was obviously taken aback.. Whatever she'd been expecting, it wasn't that. She took a good, long look at me and said, 'You're serious, aren't you?'

I nodded vigorously. 'You'd have no problem working there because you're old enough.'

'That's not the point. They probably won't be able to afford me. They only take on two helpers during the summer and Christmas holidays. They can't afford to take on a worker at any other time of the year,' Halle frowned.

'But if you tell them that you don't even want to be paid, they'll probably snatch your hand off!' I beamed at her. I'd already thought about that bit.

'Why should she want to work there if she doesn't get paid?' Nosh questioned.

'That's easy. She could say that she really believes in what ANTIDOTE are doing . . .'

'I *do* really believe in what they're doing,' Halle shot back.

'That's what makes it even better,' I told her. 'You won't have to lie.'

'So let me get this straight – I'm supposed to start working there and spy on people I already know. I'm supposed to just dig around in their filing cabinets and on their computers until I find something which might, only *might*, mind you, help your mum and your Uncle Robert. Is that right?'

I frowned. When she put it like that it did seem like a crazy idea.

'What exactly am I meant to be looking for?'

'I don't know,' I admitted. 'But there's got to be something . . .'

'What're you not telling me?' Halle's eyes narrowed.

'What d'you mean?'

'This feels like there's a whole chunk missing somewhere. No way am I even going to think about this until I know exactly what I'm letting myself in for,' Halle said.

Whatever else she was, she was nobody's fool. I didn't want to tell her the whole, full story. Suppose I told her and she still said no. But from the expression on her face she wasn't going to change her mind.

'It's . . . it's just that it could be dangerous . . .' I said reluctantly.

'Dangerous?' she said, startled.

'That's right! Yes, it could!' Nosh's eyes took on a sudden gleam of delight. 'Say you'll do it, Halle!'

'Nosh, this isn't a joke,' I told him.

'I know,' Nosh beamed devilishly, still relishing the idea of the trouble his sister could get into.

After giving Nosh the filthiest look I've ever

seen, Halle turned to me and asked, 'Just exactly how might this be dangerous? And I want the whole story or nothing doing.'

Nosh quickly shook his head at me. I had Halle's full attention. It was decision time. Should I tell her everything that was going on or not?

'D'you promise not to tell your parents or anyone? D'you promise to keep it to yourself – even if you say no?' I asked.

'Yes, of course.'

'And you won't tell your boyfriend – butt-features?!' Nosh said suspiciously.

Halle scowled at her brother then turned to me. 'You have my word, Elliot.'

So I told her. Everything.

Halle didn't interrupt me once. She started once or twice, looked at me sceptically more often than that, but she didn't interrupt. When I finished, she looked at me without blinking for a few moments.

'And that's all true?' It was more of a statement than a question.

I didn't answer. I didn't even have to nod my head.

'Why on earth don't you go to the police?'

'And tell them what?' I asked. 'That the Shelby security video tape is a fake? That someone at Shelby's is out to get my mum? They'd laugh in my face. My mum's just a secretary . . .' But even as I said it, I could hear my voice waver.

What about the conversation between Uncle Robert and Mum? She may be a secretary now but it was clear that that hadn't always been the case. 'The first question they'll ask is why would anyone at Shelby's be out to frame my mum?'

'But it doesn't necessarily have to be someone at Shelby's. From what you just said, it must be someone at ANTIDOTE,' Halle pointed out.

'I've thought of that too. But going to the police is just going to alert the Shelby agent in ANTIDOTE that we're on to them. Then we'll never find out who it is,' I replied. 'And I can't just go in and produce the Marcus Pardela memo 'cause they'd say that I made it up myself.'

'I can't believe it.' Halle's eyes blazed. 'To think that someone at ANTIDOTE works for the opposition . . . Show me this letter from Marcus Pardela that you say you printed off.'

I dug it out of my pocket and handed it over. It was pretty mangled by now. Halle held it disdainfully by one corner and started to read.

'But this isn't on your mum's PC any more?' Halle asked when she'd finished.

'There's nothing left on my mum's PC,' I said gloomily. 'It's been completely erased. If all the files had just been deleted then I could get them back but the whole disk has been unconditionally formatted. It's clean.'

'So if I do go to work for ANTIDOTE, how will I even know what to look for?'

I leaned forward eagerly. 'I thought I could re-install all Mum's software on her PC tomorrow and create a disk for you to take with you on Monday. Then you could put my disk into each person's PC and run just one file. I'd set it up so that everything else was done for you. My disk would search each computer for any information sent to or received from Marcus Pardela or that other guy – what'shisname Shelby. I'd copy all the information onto the floppy disk and all you'd have to do is bring the disk home and I'd check it here.'

'Would that work?' Halle asked doubtfully.

I sat back, indignant. 'Of course it'd work. *I'd* write it!'

'Pardon me!' Halle raised an eyebrow. 'And when exactly am I meant to load up this disk?'

'In the lunch break when there's no-one around, or after work?' I ventured.

Halle chewed on her bottom lip. She didn't look at all happy and to be honest, I couldn't blame her. It was dangerous and goodness only knew what would happen if something went wrong and she got caught. But she was my last hope.

Please don't say no. Please don't say no . . . Please don't say . . .

'OK, I'll do it. But not for you – for your mum and for ANTIDOTE. I believe in what they're doing and I wouldn't want to stand by and let anyone from Shelby's jeopardize that,' Halle said at last.

I leapt out of the chair.

'You'll do it? You'll really do it?'

'I just said so, didn't I,' Halle sniffed. 'And I'm regretting it already.'

'Thank you.' I bounded round the room, unable to keep still. 'We'll find out who the Shelby agent is and then get them to admit to the police that my mum and uncle were framed for something they didn't do. Yeepee!'

'Hold your horses.' Halle put out a hand. 'Before we start making a rabbit pie, we've got to catch our rabbit first.'

That slowed me down a bit. I *was* getting ahead of myself but it had to work, it just had to.

'OK. You sort out this disk I'm meant to use and I'll take it from there. But don't count your chickens. ANTIDOTE might not even want me to work there,' said Halle.

'Of course they will,' I grinned at her. 'You'll just have to charm them.'

'Then she doesn't stand a chance,' Nosh stage-whispered from behind me.

Both Halle and I turned around to glower at him. He shrank into the chair and shut up – for once!

12

Nine-Fifteen

Up and down, up and down. Stop and wait. Up and down. Stop and wait. On and on. And still the phone didn't ring. Admittedly, I was still a couple of minutes ahead of time. Nine-fifteen the note had said.

'Elliot, sit down for goodness' sake. You're making me dizzy,' Nosh complained. He sat halfway up the stairs, watching me.

'It's all right for you,' I glared.

'No, it isn't,' Nosh interrupted. 'We're friends, aren't we? If you're upset, I'm upset.'

I briefly smiled at him, grateful that I wasn't totally alone in all this. I sat down on the second-to-last stair and waited. I'm not very good at waiting. In fact it's one of my worst things. I'd always much rather be *doing* than watching and waiting.

The house was in darkness apart from the hall, and perfectly still. I thought about what had happened so far – what I'd done or not done, what I'd *achieved*. It didn't seem like much. But what else could I do? Halle would get a job at ANTIDOTE (hopefully) and find something to connect someone at ANTIDOTE with Shelby's and then maybe I could use that information to force the Shelby agent at ANTIDOTE to help Mum and Uncle Robert. That's all I wanted. The agent could tell the police that Mum and Uncle Robert had been framed, that they were innocent. I didn't particularly care what happened after that.

The sudden shrill ring of the phone startled me. I rushed over and snatched it up.

'Hello?'

Silence.

I tried again. 'Hello?'

The phone clicked faintly back at me.

'Hello, dear. Are you all right?'

'Mum! Oh, Mum, I'm fine. I miss you. Where are you? It's good to hear your voice.' I could feel myself choking up, even though I'd just spent the last few hours telling myself I wouldn't.

The phone line clicked again.

'Are you still staying over at Nosh's house?'

'Yes, Mum.'

'Good. Not giving them any trouble?'

'Not much,' I said, remembering what had happened earlier. 'When can I see you, Mum?'

Click . . .

'I'm working on it. I'm missing you horribly, Elliot,' Mum sighed.

'You sound tired.'

'I am tired,' Mum admitted. 'It's taking longer than I thought to try and clear my name.'

'I saw the video tape that's meant to be of you and Uncle Robert,' I said eagerly. 'You were right. It *had* been doctored.'

'Where did you see that?' Mum's voice was suddenly sharp, alert.

'At the ANTIDOTE office. They got sent one anonymously,' I began.

'Elliot, keep away from that place. D'you hear me?'

'But Mum . . .'

Click . . . There it was again.

'What's that funny clicking noise?' I asked, irritated. 'Is that something where you are?'

There was a brief pause.

'Elliot, the phone's been bugged. I can't stay on the line much longer or they'll trace the call and find me.'

'The phone's bugged?' I pulled the receiver away from my face and stared at it. I couldn't have been more stunned and shocked than if it'd just turned into a spitting cobra.

'Who bugged the phone? Was it Shelby's? And why? Why do they want to get you into trouble with the police? I don't understand. Why *you*?' I was choking up again.

'Elliot, listen. We don't have much time left. Visit your favourite spot in the park any time on Monday. I'll be waiting for you.'

'Mum?' What was she doing? If the phone really was bugged then the heavies from Shelby's would have heard every word and would surely be waiting, too?

Click . . .

'It's OK, Elliot. I know what I'm doing,' Mum told me. 'Just make sure you don't bring anything with you.'

I instantly knew what Mum meant by the way she stressed *anything*. She didn't want me to bring her organizer.

Click . . .

'Mum, are you . . . are you really just a secretary?' I whispered.

Pause.

'Elliot, I've only got a few more seconds. They'll be able to trace the call . . .'

'Are you?' I insisted.

'No.'

The phone clicked again, then went dead with a different kind of click. But my ears, my entire brain reverberated with Mum's answer to my question.

No . . .

I put down the phone, then picked up the

whole thing and put it on the floor. I don't know what I expected it to do. Maybe I expected it to morph into one of those two men who'd been outside Uncle Robert's house. All I knew was, I was afraid of it. Afraid of it for the things I learned over it.

'Did you say the phone has been bugged?' Nosh asked with breathless horror.

I turned to him and nodded, my fingers over my lips. I pointed to the phone and shook my head. Nosh got what I was trying to say at once. But even if the phone was bugged, that was nothing compared to Mum's other revelation.

She wasn't a secretary. And she was involved in something that had others interested enough in her to bug our phone.

So if Mum wasn't a secretary, what was she? I replayed the conversation I'd overheard between Mum and Uncle Robert again in my head, trying to work it out. What job was it that Mum gave up when I was born? The job that made Uncle Robert ask for her help in getting evidence of Shelby's illegal animal experiments?

It was then that I remembered the last Thursday of term in Mr Oakley's class when he'd asked us what our mothers did for a living. Hadn't I wished that Mum did something a bit more exciting than just being a secretary? Well, now I'd got my wish – only now I wished I hadn't! All this trouble had started from the time I'd made that wish in the classroom. It was almost as if I'd asked for all this chaos to descend over our heads.

'I didn't mean it,' I muttered to myself. 'I really didn't. I don't mind if Mum's a secretary. In fact, I'd prefer it.'

'What did you say?' Nosh asked.

'Nothing,' I sighed.

But it was too late. Mum wasn't a secretary. She'd said so herself and confirmed what I'd suspected over the last few days. I took a deep breath, then another which I cut off abruptly. Could the people who'd bugged our phone hear me – even now? Could they hear my breathing? Had they heard what I'd said about Mum? Did they know Nosh and I were alone in the house? I picked up the phone and looked all over the handset and the underside of it. I don't know what I expected to find. Maybe a small button-sized object with the word 'BUG' written on it in capitals!

'What're you doing?' Nosh called out.

'If the phone's bugged, they might be listening to us right now,' I replied. 'Or they could be outside, watching the house . . .'

'I don't like this . . .' Nosh's tone was an echo of my own.

I beckoned to Nosh with my finger and we

made our way into the front room. I looked through the window.

'I can't see anyone . . .' I began. 'But if they're not already outside, maybe they're on their way here now . . . ?'

'Thank you for sharing that with me,' Nosh said. 'As if I wasn't scared enough already.'

We went back to the hall. I don't know about Nosh but my heart was thumping fit to bust in my chest.

'Elliot, let's get out of here,' Nosh stage-whispered.

'Good idea,' I agreed.

I opened the front door and we left the house, slamming the door shut behind us. The road was deserted. We looked around, our heads jerking every which way until we were safely back in Nosh's house. And all the time I remembered something Mum was always saying to me – be careful what you wish for, or you just might get it!

Now for the first time, I could see exactly what she meant by that.

SUNDAY

13

Progress

I woke up just after seven o'clock Sunday morning – which was unheard of for me. To be honest I was surprised I got to sleep at all. In the half light of the dawn, I could see that Nosh was still fast asleep. I envied him. I lay perfectly still, staring up at the ceiling. In a strange way, I was calmer and more together than I'd felt in a long, long time. Only one more day and then I'd see Mum again. Only one more day and then I'd learn exactly what was going on and what all this was about. How I wished it was Monday already. But half an hour of wishing seemed to make Sunday morning pass even more slowly. I couldn't spend Sunday doing nothing.

Come on, I told myself. Get up and do something!

The trouble was, I spent at least an hour in bed doing exactly nothing as I tried to make up my mind what I should do with the rest of the day. Luckily, Nosh's mum came to my rescue soon afterwards. I heard her up and about and reckoned that in less than an hour she'd be calling Nosh and me downstairs for our breakfast. I wasn't wrong.

As soon as I'd wolfed down my breakfast I wanted to go back to my own house for a while. Nosh's mum wasn't too happy about me going home by myself, but I wasn't going to let that stop me.

'Why don't you wait for Nosh? Then you can go over together,' she suggested.

I shook my head. 'It's my house. I don't want to feel that it's not safe unless I've got someone with me,' I told her.

She sighed, but gave in after that.

'HELLO?' I shouted once I'd got home, even though I knew that no-one was there. The silence in the house echoed back at me. 'MUM?' I shouted again.

After a deep breath, I told myself not to be such a coward. There was no-one in the house. No Mum and no burglars. All I was doing was whistling in the dark in the vain hope that if there *was* someone in the house – apart from Mum – then they would leg it out the back at the sound of my voice. With determined heavy footsteps, I made my way up the stairs and into the back bedroom. I switched on Mum's PC, then dug out Uncle Robert's back-up tape. But first I had to load up all the utility software, like the operating system and all the software required to make the CD player, the scanner, the printer and all the other devices attached to Mum's PC work. Only after that did I load Uncle's tape, typing in the necessary <RESTORE> command, before sitting back and waiting.

But I couldn't sit still. The house was too quiet. I went into my bedroom to get my CD/radio player and took it into the back bedroom with me. The CD of Michael Jackson's *Dangerous* was still in there and I didn't bother to change it. I pressed the play button and turned up the volume, feeling slightly silly at being so nervous, but doing it nonetheless. Michael Jackson was well into the third song on the CD before the tape had finished downloading. It was ridiculously slow! With impatient fingers I began to hunt through Uncle Robert's system, unsure of what I was looking for but hoping that something would jump out at me. There were a number of ANTIDOTE directories, full of memos, letters and documents written by various people in the ANTIDOTE office, but nothing that looked out of the ordinary. Searching through the hard disk was like looking for a needle in a haystack. Harder in fact, because I had no idea what the needle looked like or even if it was there at all.

Two hours later, I was burning with frustration at my lack of success. I'd learnt more about ANTIDOTE than I'd ever wanted. I knew who was due for a pay rise, all about the office furniture re-shuffle and had read proposal documents on the previous day's march to Shelby's. But there was nothing about the mole in the company, nor anything else that could help me. There were two memos – from Uncle Robert to Sarah Irving and vice versa – listing dates, times and ports where ANTIDOTE were sure Shelby's had illegally smuggled in animals for their experiments – but even that didn't help much because the dates were all in the past. Then an idea hit me. There was still one place I hadn't searched.

Uncle's Internet account . . . I had his user ID and password, so why not? Uncle wouldn't mind – not once he knew why I'd done it. I switched on the modem and then logged on to Uncle's Internet account. After selecting the <GET NEW MAIL> option, the screen cleared and then:

```
                  You have 4 new mail messages:
Subject:                            Sender      Size    Importance   Status
Shelby Protest March                SIrving     2272    Urgent       Unread
Deleting Old Mail Messages - Please! RAdjava    77623   Important    Unread
Toxic Waste Dumping - New Evidence  SIrving     3980    Normal       Unread
The New Office Fax Machine          IMacmillan  2075    Important    Unread
```

'Yes!' I grinned.

At last – progress!

But when I checked through the e-mail messages, they were all as dry as stale biscuits. I sat back and frowned at the screen. There had to be something else I could do. I was on the right track. I could *feel* it, but now what? I decided to check through the log of all Uncle's incoming e-mail messages – all the ones he'd received from other people. I expected to see a list of about a dozen or so messages but it looked like Uncle had kept every message he'd ever been sent from the time the Internet had started! I searched down through his list, starting with the most recent message first. I checked each subject heading carefully but nothing jumped out at me. I only went back over the last month. I reckoned Uncle must have found out about the mole at ANTI-DOTE quite recently so there was no point in going back beyond that date. He and the others at ANTIDOTE wouldn't want to hang around doing nothing once they knew that one of them was a traitor. I went back to the beginning and checked both the subject heading and the sender details in case I'd missed something.

Nothing.

I was about to give up and load Mum's back-up tape when it occurred to me that I hadn't checked down the list of messages that

Uncle Robert had sent out. I frowned as I considered. Was it even worth doing this? I really was clutching at straws now. Deciding that I might as well, just to be thorough, I called up the list and glanced down it.

Robert Gaines - Outgoing Messages:			
Subject: Message No:	Recipient	Date	Status
Shelby Protest March 288392903	SIrving	11 Apr	Normal
Animal Experiments At Shelby's 484400282	RAdjava,IMacmillan SIrving, PPatrick	11 Apr	Urgent
Toxic Waste Dumping 273402586	SIrving,IMacmillan RAdjava	11 Apr	Important
183404292		11 Apr	Confidential
The New Office Fax Machine 936404397	IMacmillan	9 Apr	Normal
A Decent Chair For My Bad Back 483855780	SIrving,AJones	7 Apr	Important
Cyanide Dumping In River Tay 748574920	SIrving,RAdjava, PPatrick,DGraves, JHeinmann	5 Apr	Important
Staff And Salary Review 347394034	SIrving	4 Apr	Confidential
Turn Off The Lights At Night 598304403	General Office	30 Apr	Normal

Screen 1 of 150

I noticed it at once because *it wasn't there*. There was a list of all the e-mail messages Uncle Robert had sent out in the last month and he'd carefully kept copies of each of them – except one. The e-mail message number was still listed but there was no heading and no recipient details. Why would Uncle not input the details to just that one message?

I made a note of the e-mail message number on the back of my hand, then downloaded Mum's back-up tape. I went straight into her Internet account to check her incoming e-mail messages. Like Uncle, she had a list of all her incoming messages going back over the last three months. But there was one message which had no sender or subject heading details. I checked the message number – 183404292. It was the same message that Uncle Robert had sent out. I tried to call up the message by double-clicking on the right line but the warning,

```
Error. E-mail message number 183404292,
                not available
```

appeared. I had a quick scan through all Mum's other directories and likely-looking files on the hard disk but again, nothing else leapt out at me.

So where was this missing e-mail message? After a moment's thought, I checked the history log for 11th April. The history log was a log of all the commands Mum had typed in on that day and the log filled at least five screens. I searched through it carefully, until I came to the line that explained what had happened to the file.

Mum had copied the mail message onto her organizer, making sure that the message would be deleted once it'd been copied. And that would certainly explain why both Mum and Uncle Robert's hard disks had been trashed and why Smiler and his friend were so keen to get hold of Mum's organizer.

But what did this mail message say? Was it to do with ANTIDOTE.CONFIDENTIAL, the file that Marcus Pardela had sent to his colleague in Geneva? I dismissed the idea at once. I couldn't believe Marcus Pardela and his cronies would go to all this trouble over that memo.

So it had to be something else. If it was important before, it was even more urgent now that I break Mum's password on her organizer and find the message. I was going to spend the rest of Sunday trying to crack the password and I *was* going to do it – I had to believe that.

But first things first. I had to write the program to search each of the PCs at the ANTIDOTE office. I'd probably only get one shot at this so I had to get it right.

I spent the rest of the morning and all of the

afternoon writing and testing my program. I tested it using Uncle Robert's back-up tape as well as Mum's. My program searched through all the text files on the hard disk looking for certain words. Any file with those words in it was copied to the floppy disk. When I was happy it was working, I loaded the program onto a floppy disk that I could give to Halle. Then I realized I'd have to set up another disk for Halle. That took me another hour, but it was worth it because then I knew we were all set.

I switched off the PC and headed back to Nosh's house, taking a good look around me once I was outside. The chills tingling up and down my spine like icy fingers made me hurry. Once I was at Nosh's door, I had another look around. There was no-one in sight – but I knew, just as surely as I knew my own name – that I was being watched.

MONDAY

14

Julian

Sunday turned into Monday and I think I had
Mum's organizer out of my hands for all of
about ten minutes. I even slept with it in my
hand, with my hand under my pillow. I
wouldn't let the thing out of my sight. I reckoned that with me at all times was the safest
place for it. I tried everything I could think of
but I still had no luck cracking Mum's code.
The only other way of getting into the organizer was to reset it. That would wipe out
Mum's password all right. The only trouble
was, it would wipe out all the other data on
the organizer as well, which was the last thing
I wanted.

And I had an even bigger concern. Today
was the day when I was meant to meet Mum
in the park. And – if Mum was right about our
phone being bugged – she wouldn't be the
only one waiting for me.

Throughout breakfast, I hardly said a word.
I forced myself to eat and try to appear

normal, but my bacon could've been gravel for all the pleasure I got from eating it.

'Are you sure you're all right?' Nosh's mum asked me more than once.

I just nodded before returning to the organizer screen.

Halle's boyfriend, Julian, came around at about half-nine. I was the one who was unlucky enough to open the door for him. He was gangly and skinny and spotty and had a really fake grin plastered over his face. He was what Uncle Robert would call a tall glass of warm water! His hair must have had a whole can of mousse sprayed into it, as each thin section of hair was carefully combed back and defined and it was a colour I'd never seen before, a strange kind of charcoal grey. His eyes were the same colour too which made me suspect his hair colour was out of a bottle.

'Hi!' he smiled. 'You must be one of Nosh's little friends.'

I didn't say a word. One of Nosh's little friends, indeed! What a bloomin' cheek!

'Is Halle in?' he asked, still grinning at me.

'Halle, your boyfriend, Hadrian, is here,' I shouted.

'The name is Julian,' he corrected.

'Whatever!' I dismissed and walked off leaving him at the door.

What a Cedric! Nosh was absolutely right

about him. Halle dashed down the stairs, almost knocking me over in her hurry to get to 'Julian'.

'Elliot, his name is Julian not Hadrian – as I'm sure you know. You won't be so cute if you start picking up Nosh's bad habits,' frowned Halle.

'I don't have to pick up anyone's bad habits. I've got enough of my own,' I told her.

She flounced past me, unimpressed and started kissing Julian on the doorstep. I thought they were trying to swallow each other. It was disgusting! Leaving them to it, I started up the stairs. With a sudden start, I turned back.

'Halle, you are still going to help me, aren't you?' I asked quickly.

'I said so, didn't I?' Halle replied. 'Don't nag me. I hate to be nagged.'

Me? Nag? I felt like telling her that only grown-ups nagged, but I didn't push it. Today was definitely a day when things were going to happen. But I'd given up trying to predict if they were good things or bad things. My gut feelings had let me down before – and in a big way. I dug the floppies out of my pocket and went back downstairs, followed by Nosh who suddenly appeared. Halle and Julian were holding hands and gazing into each other's eyes. If they knew how drippy they looked, they wouldn't have done it!

'Halle, here's the first disk I was telling you about,' I said pointedly.

Puzzled, Halle frowned at me, then her expression cleared. 'Oh, yes! So what do I do with it?' she asked.

'You load it up on each PC you can and just type A:DETECT,' I told her.

'A:DETECT,' Halle repeated. 'Got it.'

I handed her a second disk. 'You load up this disk on each PC and type A:E-MAIL.'

'What does this disk do?' Halle frowned.

'It will copy each person's e-mail directory onto the floppy. All the files will be copied across – including each person's e-mail set-up file which includes their password. That way I can read everyone's mail without having to worry about breaking their passwords. I've just about had enough of trying to break people's passwords!'

Halle chewed on her bottom lip, her unease evident. 'I must admit, Elliot, I'm not so sure about this any more . . .'

'Not so sure about what, muffin?' Julian asked.

Muffin! *Ple-eease!*

'Pass the sick bucket.' Nosh said what I was thinking.

'Haven't you got something better to do,

Nosh?' asked Halle. 'Like playing with the traffic?'

'Only if you join me,' said Nosh, sweetly.

'Not so sure about what, muffin?' Julian repeated.

'I'm coming with you to the ANTIDOTE office,' I told Halle.

'Oh, no you're not. I can't do this with you trailing behind me. How would I explain your presence? And besides, I'm quite capable of doing this on my own.'

'Doing what?' asked Julian.

'One of us should be with you, in case you get into trouble,' said Nosh reluctantly.

'And what could you do, squirt?' Halle said, dismissively. 'I'm quite capable of looking after myself.'

'Would someone please tell me what's going on?' Julian asked, exasperated.

Halle looked at me. 'Can I tell him?'

I shook my head slowly. I didn't want anyone else to know what was going on – and especially not Julian. I mean, he was a total Cedric and then some! It had been hard enough bringing Halle in on this. If I could've thought of a way of getting the information off the PCs at the ANTIDOTE office without involving her, believe me, I would've.

'Please let me tell him,' said Halle. 'Julian could come with me and help out. Besides, if it might be at all dangerous, wouldn't we all feel better if I didn't go alone?'

'I thought you just said you could handle yourself,' Nosh reminded her.

'I can,' Halle snapped back. 'But it wouldn't hurt to have Julian along, now would it?'

'Halle, what're you getting yourself into?' Julian's eyes narrowed suspiciously.

Halle looked at me pointedly. I frowned at her. As I turned to Julian I could feel my frown deepening. Now what? Halle was right about Julian being able to back her up. And I'd never forgive myself if something bad happened to Halle because of me.

'Oh, all right then,' I sighed.

Halle smiled at me. 'It'll be OK. You can trust Julian. He's grade A.'

I caught Nosh's derisive snort even if Halle didn't. She told Julian the whole story and far more succinctly than I had. I watched his face intently as Halle spoke, trying to gauge his reaction. He looked . . . almost shocked. He couldn't have been more stunned if it was his own mother and uncle Halle was talking about. Then his expression seemed to clear and he looked at me, disbelieving, as if he thought I was making the whole thing up to steal his girlfriend or something.

'It's true. Every word,' I told him.

'I never said it wasn't,' Julian replied.

'I saw the look on your face,' I said.

'It didn't mean what you think it meant,' Julian said, adding bitterly, 'I'd believe anything you said about Shelby's. I wouldn't put anything past Marcus Pardela.' He turned to Halle. 'Well, you're definitely not going to the ANTIDOTE office by yourself. I'm coming with you.'

'I hoped you'd say that.' Halle beamed at him.

I was in no position to argue, but I couldn't help being a bit peeved at Halle. It was as if this whole exercise was just another way for her to get together with Julian. Don't get me wrong, I *was* grateful, but it felt like Mum and me were a poor second on Halle's list of priorities after her boyfriend. Totally unreasonable, I know, but that's how I felt and I'd be lying if I said otherwise.

'And what happens if we do find some evidence of who the mole at ANTIDOTE is?' Julian asked.

'We use the information to get Mum and my Uncle Robert out of trouble,' I replied tersely.

What a stupid question! What did he think we'd do with the evidence? Why did he think I was doing all this?

'And how exactly do we do that?' Julian persisted.

I frowned at him, not quite sure what he was getting at.

'Are you going to go to the police, or challenge the mole directly, or try to get to Marcus Pardela with the information?' Julian expanded.

'I thought I could talk to the Shelby agent at ANTIDOTE directly,' I said.

'And what happens if the Shelby agent tells you to do your worst, or just doesn't care?' asked Julian. 'I'm sure Marcus Pardela has already made plans just in case his mole at ANTIDOTE is found out.'

I hadn't thought of that and it showed on my face.

'You obviously don't play chess,' Julian said. 'If you did, you'd know how important it is to think more than one move ahead. That way you don't get caught out.'

He had a point.

'OK, then. Tell us what we should do once we get the information – if you're so clever,' Nosh challenged.

'You have to come up with alternative plans of action. That's all I'm saying,' said Julian.

'I think that once we get proof of who the agent is, we should go straight to the top – Marcus Pardela. We should tell him that he's got to admit that the video tape of Elliot's mum and uncle is a fake or we'll publicize the fact that he put a spy into ANTIDOTE,' Halle said decisively.

'And you really think a man like Pardela would be scared of that?' Julian snorted. 'He'd just laugh in your face.'

'You don't know that,' Halle argued.

'Oh yes, I do,' Julian's reply was immediate.

'Do you know Marcus Pardela, then?' Halle said, surprised.

'I know his type.' Julian's voice had a strange edge to it. 'Believe me, he doesn't care about anyone or anything but himself and his company. Even if we do find out who the Shelby spy at ANTIDOTE is, Marcus Pardela will just remove him or her and put someone else in their place.'

'So what would you suggest?' asked Halle.

'Elliot, where's this confidential memo of yours sent from Marcus Pardela to Joshua Shelby?' Julian asked.

I dug it out of my pocket. As Julian reached out for it, I quickly pulled my hand back.

'Why d'you want it?' I asked, suspiciously.

'Well, for one thing, I can see it's falling apart – so I'll make several photocopies of it as our record of what was said. And for another, I've got a idea how we can use this to flush out our mole – that is, assuming that they let Halle and me work there in the first place.'

'Why do you want to help? You don't know me or my family.' I still wasn't sure about Julian. I agreed with everything he'd said, but, I don't know – there was something about him . . .

'I don't need to know every last detail about you to want to help, do I?' Julian shrugged. 'And besides, anything I can do to help ANTIDOTE against Shelby and Pardela Pharmaceuticals is fine with me.'

I handed over the memo.

'How do we use the memo to get to the double agent, then?' Nosh asked, his eyes gleaming.

'You leave that to me. Halle, we need to stop off at my flat first. I've got some things to set up before we go to the ANTIDOTE office,' said Julian.

'Like what?' I asked.

'I won't say – in case it doesn't work,' Julian replied. 'Just stay out of trouble until we get back tonight.'

Stay out of trouble! That was a joke. I was going to the park to see Mum, and goodness only knew who else would be there.

'Hang on a minute,' Nosh glowered at Julian. 'You can't just decide to take over . . .'

'Come on, Nosh. We've got some other

things to sort out,' I interrupted him.

'What will you two be doing until we get back?' Julian asked, his expression speculative.

'We're going to the park,' I told him.

'Hhmm! That's all right, then,' he smiled.

I went upstairs to Nosh's room. Reluctantly, he followed me.

'Who does Julian think he is?' he exploded once the door was closed. 'He only just found out about all this two seconds ago and now he wants to run the whole show . . .'

'Listen, Nosh. If Julian can help us then I'm not going to stop him. If nothing else, this whole business has taught me that I can't do everything myself. I just can't,' I said. 'And Julian was right about planning ahead, so that's exactly what I intend to do.'

'Plan ahead for what?' Nosh asked.

I took a deep breath. 'Mum wants me to meet her today.'

'Where?'

'At the park.'

'When?'

'She didn't specify a time.'

'When did she tell you this?'

'Over the phone on Saturday night.'

Nosh stared at me. 'Wait a sec. I thought you told me that your mum reckoned your phone was bugged.'

'That's right,' I replied.

Nosh was astounded. 'And she still made arrangements to meet you at the park?'

I nodded.

'I don't understand.'

'Neither do I. But that's what she wanted me to do. I'm supposed to meet Mum at my favourite spot in the park,' I remembered.

'And where's that?' asked Nosh.

'I don't have one.'

'But your mum was the one who suggested the meeting place, wasn't she?' Nosh looked perplexed.

'Yeah, I don't understand that either,' I admitted. 'I hate the park. I've told Mum that often enough . . .' I stared at Nosh. 'What an idiot!'

'Who is?'

'I am,' I replied. 'I'm so *slow*. Of course.'

'Elliot, you're getting on my nerves now,' Nosh said, irritated. 'What're you going on about?'

'Mum doesn't want me to go to the park at all.' Only now did I remember the conversation I'd had with Mum just before Uncle Robert had arrived last week.

Mum wanted me to meet her at the fish and chip shop opposite.

'I've got one thing to do first and then I'm going to need your help – just in case I am being watched and followed.'

'What d'you want me to do?' Nosh asked.

'It'll be dangerous . . .' I warned him.

'So what else is new?' Nosh said dryly.

'I need you to be me.'

Once I'd told Nosh my plan, his expression was the most serious I'd ever seen it.

'Elliot,' he said quietly. 'We're getting deeper and deeper into this and we'll be lucky to find our way out again.'

And how could I argue with him?

'D'you want to back out?' I asked, my heart in my throat.

'Yes,' he replied at once. 'But I'm not going to.'

I took a deep breath to steady my nerves. It didn't work. 'Let's get going,' I said. 'Before we both change our minds.'

15

True Colours

'Are you just going to stand there collecting dust or are you actually going to buy something?'

I glared at Tony behind the counter. Sarky old trout!

'I'll have a bag of chips, please,' I said, after studying the menu board behind him.

'Is that all?'

I nodded.

'Why has it taken you over half an hour to decide on a bag of chips?' he asked, annoyed.

'I was waiting for you to bring out a fresh batch of chips,' I improvised.

Tony gave an exaggerated sigh and looked distinctly cheesed off. What was his problem? It was the middle of the afternoon, for goodness' sake! The lunchtime rush was over and the early dinner crush hadn't yet started, so why was he giving me grief? As he served up one portion of chips, I had another look around.

Where was Mum?

And what about Nosh? Was he OK? Nosh had left the house dressed in my jacket and a woolly hat and made for the park about fifteen minutes before I'd left the house. I told him to keep his head down and not look up at anyone for at least an hour. Right now he should be making yet another circuit of the park, watched by goodness only knew who. But if they were watching him, they wouldn't be watching me. I just hoped that Nosh would be all right.

I glanced down at my watch. Mum hadn't specified a time, so I had no way of knowing when she might arrive.

'D'you want these chips or not?'

I turned back to Tony behind the counter. Someone had obviously woken up on the wrong side of bed this morning.

I handed over my money and got my chips. Moving to one side of the shop, I leaned against the wall and stood there eating my chips one at a time as I looked out of the shop window.

'This isn't a restaurant, you know,' Tony snapped.

'Oh, go on, mister. It's raining outside. Couldn't I just stay here until it stops? You do the best chips for miles. You wouldn't want me to get them all soggy and spoil them, would you?!'

Tony regarded me. His lips twitched. 'Oh, all right, then. But as soon as you've finished eating, off you go.'

I smiled gratefully and carried on looking out of the shop window. I had got it right, hadn't I? Mum did mean for me to meet her here? Suppose I was trying to be too clever and Mum really had meant for me to meet her in the park. I shook my head. No, I must've got it right. I was just panicking, that's all. I couldn't stay in the chip shop for ever and if I went outside, there was the chance that I might be spotted. I nibbled each chip really slowly, chewing on each mouthful a good thirty times before swallowing. I was determined to stay put for as long as possible.

I watched the street as people came and went in the chip shop. I was totally focused on seeing Mum, no-one else. And yet when I did catch sight of her, it was still a shock. She emerged from the back of a car which had Drive-Rite Mini Cars painted in big letters down its side. The mini-cab drove off immediately. Mum stood across the street, looking into the chip shop. She was wearing a raincoat with the collar turned up against the weather, and a flat cap. She just stood there looking into the shop, even though I must've been visible at the window. With a burst of pure joy, I headed for the door. Mum started across the street.

'Oh, hello, Elliot. This is a surprise.'

I almost collided with the man who had spoken to me. I gasped with dismay. It was Smiler – the man with the ponytail who'd been waiting outside Uncle Robert's house. And whatever else this was, it was no chance meeting.

'Where're you going in such a hurry?' Smiler smiled, silkily.

I glanced across the street. Smiler's eyes followed mine. His smile instantly vanished. Mum stood stock still in the middle of the road. A car rushed past her, the driver honking his horn indignantly.

I tried to run out of the shop but Smiler was out before me. Mum raced off down the street, closely followed by Smiler with me trailing behind both of them.

'MUM! MUM, RUN!' I yelled.

'Elliot, get out of here!' Mum turned her head to call back to me.

No way was I going to leave her now. Mum turned the corner pursued by Smiler who was gaining on her. I turned the corner just in time to see Mum dart across the road towards the same mini-cab that had dropped her off. The cab was driving slowly, its back door open.

Mum practically dived into the car which then took off, its accelerator roaring.

I tried to see who the driver was but what with the rain and the windscreen wipers and the speed the car was going, I couldn't see a thing. The car whizzed by too quickly.

Smiler stood in the middle of the street, intense fury on his face – his true colours revealed. His hands were clenched so tightly into fists that I could see the veins standing out on the back of his hands. He scowled down the street after the mini-cab, the muscles in his neck standing out like old rope. He turned to face me. If looks were made of fire, I would've been a mere shadow on the ground. He started coming towards me, ignoring the cars whistling past him.

With each step he took towards me, I took a wary step backwards. Our eyes were locked together. I didn't even dare blink. I was a rabbit, caught in a car's headlights. But then Smiler started running.

I may be a lot of things but I'm no mug. I turned and ran for my life – and that's just exactly what it felt like. Like I was running for my life.

16

Watching And Waiting

I ran all the way home, not daring to look back once. My calves felt like white-hot pokers were being thrust into them, I thought my lungs were going to burst, and my blood was pounding so hard around my body that I could barely hear the traffic around me, but still I kept going. It was only when I stood in front of Nosh's house that I stopped and looked around. Smiler was nowhere in sight. I don't know when he'd decided to give up chasing me. It could have been five seconds after I started running, it could've been only five seconds ago – but I was alone. I rang the doorbell and practically fell into the house when Nosh's mum opened the door.

'Elliot! Are you all right?' she asked, as I stumbled past her.

I nodded. I couldn't speak. I was fighting to get my breath back.

'Elliot, what's the matter? You're wheezing

like the devil himself was chasing you,' said Nosh's mum.

I shook my head, still gasping for breath.

'I'm fine,' I gasped. 'I just decided to run for a while.'

Nosh's mum frowned. 'You're meant to start slowly and build up. Not try to run a marathon the first time out.'

'I'll remember that for next time,' I coughed.

I dragged myself upstairs, knowing that Nosh's mum was still watching me. I headed straight for the bathroom where I was horribly, wretchedly, embarrassingly sick. I vomited up every bit of chip in my stomach. It was so bad, I'm sure I vomited up food I'd eaten as a toddler. The combination of nerves, fear and all that running had just about done me in. Once it was over, I rinsed out my mouth and washed my face. Muscles I didn't even know I had ached. I sat down, leaning against the bath tub as I tried to get my thoughts in some sort of order.

I'd been so close. *So close* . . .

Mum had been a couple of metres away and yet I'd failed again. Shelby's must have had people not just in the park, but staked out all around it.

The park . . . *Nosh* . . .

My eyes opened wide in horror. Nosh. I'd

forgotten all about him. Was he all right? Had Smiler or one of his colleagues caught him? I had to find him, I just had to. I ran downstairs and to the front door. I had the door open when Nosh's mum stepped out of the front room.

'Elliot,' she frowned. 'Where're you going?'

'I thought I'd go and find Nosh,' I said, desperate to keep any trace of panic out of my voice.

'Where is he?' Nosh's mum asked.

'He went to the park.'

'I think he can find his way home from the park OK, don't you?' she smiled.

'I could go and meet him if you like,' I tried.

'No, I don't think so,' Nosh's mum said. 'You can wait here for him.'

'Oh, but . . .'

Nosh's mum looked at me pointedly. 'Is something wrong?'

I shook my head quickly. 'No, I . . . No.'

'Then you can help me make the dinner,' she smiled.

And what could I do? The only way out of it was to tell Nosh's mum the truth and I couldn't do that – not until I knew for sure that Nosh *was* in trouble. It was cowardly I know but part of it was because I didn't want to worry her unnecessarily – and that's true. I wasn't just thinking about myself.

Nosh's mum set me to work peeling potatoes but after I'd nicked my fingers for the third time with the knife, she decided to give me something 'a little less dangerous' – as she put it. So I was put in charge of the salad, rinsing lettuce and grating carrots. If anything, the grater was more dangerous than the knife had been! It was just that I couldn't concentrate on anything I was doing. All I could think about was Nosh. I'd been wrong before when I thought that Nosh was the one who had all the imagination. My imagination was working overtime, and each thought as to what might have happened to Nosh was more dreadful than the last. Nosh's dad arrived home from work and Nosh still hadn't turned up.

'You're sure he went to the park?' Nosh's mum asked me.

I nodded. 'I'm sure he'll be home soon.'

'He'd better be,' Nosh's mum muttered under her breath.

After I'd helped prepare the dinner, I sat down in the armchair in the front room where I could see directly out of the front window. Nosh's mum and dad were watching the early evening news. Once or twice I caught Nosh's mum giving me a funny look, and more than once her eyes drifted to the clock above the mantelpiece. Glancing down at my watch, I decided to give Nosh fifteen more minutes. After that I'd tell his mum and dad everything and let them call the police. There was no way Nosh should be this late back.

But just then, I heard a key turn in the front door. I was on my feet in a second. Nosh's mum was only just behind me as I ran out into the hall.

It was Nosh.

'Where've you been? I was worried sick!' I ranted at him.

'Nosh, what time do you call this?' his mum frowned.

'Have you been in the park all this time?' I asked.

'You could've phoned to let me know what was happening,' his mum continued.

As Nosh listened to us, his head moved from left to right and back again as if he was watching a tennis match.

'So what happened?' I asked.

'What's going on?' his mum said.

'Whoa! Please!' Nosh put his hands up defensively. 'I just went for a walk in the park and I forgot all about the time.'

'Why are you wearing Elliot's jacket?' Nosh's mum asked suspiciously.

'He said I could borrow it,' Nosh said.

'Yes, I did,' I backed him up.

I looked at Nosh. He was glaring at me.

'Hhmm! Go and wash your hands. You're just in time for dinner,' Nosh's mum said.

Nosh marched upstairs in an obvious huff. I followed him.

'So how did it go?' I asked, once we were alone.

'What was all that at the door?' Nosh rounded on me. 'Mum's bad enough without you joining in as well.'

'Sorry. I was worried about you, that's all.'

'Well, don't go on at me like that again,' Nosh ordered. 'I don't like it.'

'I promise,' I said. 'Now, how did it go?'

'I walked round and round the park until my feet were covered in blisters, that's how it went,' Nosh complained. 'What about you?'

'I came this close.' I held my thumb and index finger together. 'This close to talking to Mum but that guy with the pony-tail was there, too. He chased Mum and then tried to chase me.'

Nosh stared at me. 'What happened to your mum?'

'She hopped in the back of a mini-cab and it sped off.'

'And what about you?'

'I raced all the way home,' I admitted, sheepishly. 'No way was he going to catch me.'

'How did he know you were going to be in

the fish and chip shop?' Nosh asked.

I shook my head. 'He might have seen me through the shop window. Or maybe he popped in there for a quick bag of chips. I don't know. All I do know is once again, I still haven't managed to speak to Mum.'

'What about your uncle?' Nosh asked.

'He wasn't released. He's been remanded in custody,' I replied, glumly. 'Your mum phoned up for me earlier today.'

'Remanded in custody? Why didn't they let him out?' Nosh asked.

'He's been up before magistrates before. It's always because of ANTIDOTE protest marches or demonstrations, but I guess they decided to keep him in until his court date,' I sighed.

'Maybe we'll have better luck once Halle comes home,' said Nosh.

I just hoped he was right.

17

The Mole Unmasked

The moment Halle set foot through the door, I was at her side.

'Did ANTIDOTE take you on? Did my programs work? Did you get the information we need?' I asked impatiently.

'Hello to you, too, Elliot,' Halle said dryly. Julian followed her into the house, closing the front door behind him.

'Did you get it?' I asked again. I wasn't in the mood to be teased – not after the afternoon I'd just had.

'I got some of it. I couldn't get to Rohan Adjava's PC because he was in the office all day and never away from his desk for long enough,' Halle said, handing over the disks.

'But you ran the programs on Sarah's and Ian's machines?'

'Yes. And it wasn't easy either. I had to pretend I wanted to work late and volunteer to type up flyers on Sarah's machine. Then I had to pretend that Sarah's machine wasn't working and use Ian's PC. Ian and Sarah popped in and out of the office all day. The whole thing has added an extra ten years to my life.'

'At least your years have caught up with your face, then,' Nosh told her.

I was barely listening. To be honest, I didn't much care how she'd got the data, just as long as she had.

'Halle, you had it easy,' Julian told her. 'At least they didn't use you as a general dogsbody. If I never see another box of ANTI-DOTE flyers, it'll be too soon.'

'You had the easy bit. If I'd been caught . . .'

'Easy bit?' Julian said indignantly. 'What about amending the memo and . . .'

'Come on, Nosh,' I whispered. 'Let's leave them to it.'

'Mum, Elliot and I are just popping next door,' Nosh called out.

'What about your din . . . ?'

Nosh and I were out the door before his mum could say anything else. In my house, we dashed up the stairs and I switched on Mum's PC.

'Let's hope the information we're after isn't on Rohan's machine.' Nosh crossed his fingers.

Once the PC had booted up, I loaded the DETECT floppy disk Halle had brought back. Before I could do anything else, the doorbell rang. It made both Nosh and me jump. Without saying a word to each other, we crept down the stairs. There were two silhouettes outside the front door.

'Elliot? Is that you? Open up!' It was Halle.

'What d'you want?' I called out to her.

'You don't think I did all that for nothing, do you?' she called back. 'I did all the hard work. The least you could do is let me see if it worked.'

'Don't let her in,' Nosh commanded.

It was tempting, but in the end I opened the door, saying to Nosh, 'After all, she did help us and she didn't have to.'

Halle and Julian came into the house.

'Come on then, Elliot. What're you waiting for?' Julian grinned at me.

We all went back upstairs. I ran another program I'd written on the hard disk to decompress all the data on the floppy and load it onto Mum's hard disk where there was more space. Basically, what I'd done was search for any documents containing either SHELBY or PARDELA or MARCUS or JOSHUA or PHARMACEUTICALS. And I wasn't disappointed. The floppy disk was now full.

'Don't you want to hear how I've set the ball rolling?' Julian asked me. 'I used several copies of that Marcus Pardela memo to good effect.'

I froze as my heart skipped a beat. I turned to him, dreading to hear the answer but needing to ask the question. 'What did you do?'

'I hope you didn't ruin everything,' Nosh frowned.

'Of course not,' Julian replied. 'If anything, I've speeded things up. This lunchtime, I left a copy of Marcus Pardela's memo on Sarah's, Ian's and Rohan's desks.'

It was worse than I thought.

'Why on earth did you do that?' Even Halle was astounded.

'You maggot-brain! Now the mole will know we're on to him or her!' Nosh raged.

Me? I couldn't speak. My throat was being choked from the inside. How could he? How could Julian ruin everything like this?

'No, you don't understand,' Julian said quickly. 'I amended each memo first so that it looked like the memo was copied to each individual person.'

'I don't understand,' said Halle.

Julian took a pristine, folded copy of the memo out of his jacket pocket and held it up to all of us. 'You see that "cc:" line? On one copy, I filled that in with Sarah Irving's name and left the memo on her desk. On the second copy I added Rohan's name, and on the third copy I added Ian's name. Each of them will think that the memo has been copied exclusively to them.'

The sick feeling in the pit of my stomach began to fade. I began to see what Julian had been trying to do.

'But if it was copied exclusively to them, why didn't they get the message via their e-mail? Won't they be suspicious about the fact that it's a printed copy of the memo?' I asked.

'That's the whole point,' Julian grinned. 'Two of them will wonder what's going on. But one of them – our mole – will think that somehow their message got intercepted. He or she will worry that someone else in the office is definitely on to them. All three of them were in the office this afternoon so I know they've all seen the memo. Halle didn't load up your program on Sarah and Ian's PCs until just before we came home, so if either of them panicked and sent a message to Marcus Pardela, you should have it on your e-mail floppy.'

'I'll look through that one first, then,' I said.

I took out the DETECT disk and loaded up the E-MAIL disk. I copied Sarah's and Ian's e-mail files into two different directories and then switched on the modem.

'Here goes!' I said hopefully.

I connected up to the Internet using Ian's e-mail account first. I'd been right. He had his account set up so that the user identification and password were sent out automatically, without him having to type them in each time. I was into his e-mail account just like that. I opened his out-tray and began to search through all the messages he'd sent out today. There was nothing out of the ordinary and certainly nothing to or about Marcus Pardela. Disappointed, I then went into Sarah's e-mail account. I couldn't believe she'd be the mole. She was always slagging off Shelby's.

But I was wrong.

The last e-mail message she'd sent out was to Marcus Pardela. We all looked at each other but said nothing. I retrieved the message and everyone crowded around for a closer look.

ANTIDOTE PRESSURE GROUP

Electronic Memo: Page 1 of 1

To: Marcus Pardela - MPARDELA
From: Sarah Irving - SIRVING
cc:
Status: Strictly Confidential

SUBJECT: COVER

I'm afraid I have bad news. My cover has been
blown. This afternoon I found a copy of your
confidential memo (sent to Joshua Shelby and
copied to me) on my desk. It was obviously a
warning but I don't know who left it there.
I don't think whoever it was knows anything else
but I think I should back out. I await your
further instructions.

The silence in the room was deafening.
Even though we all knew that someone at
ANTIDOTE was a traitor, it was still a shock
to see it like that.

'What a rat!' Halle fumed. 'No, she's
lower than a rat. She's a rat's bum! We should
let the others at ANTIDOTE know
immediately.'

'No, we can't,' I said quickly. 'Not until we
get my mum and Uncle Robert out of
trouble.'

'Sarah Irving.' Julian whistled. 'And she's
the ANTIDOTE spokesperson. Nine times
out of ten when ANTIDOTE are mentioned
on the telly, they show Sarah's face.'

'Can you imagine what will happen if all this
comes out? ANTIDOTE will be finished,'
Halle said. 'No more funding. No more
support. Nothing.'

'And that's probably what Pardela is relying
on,' said Julian. 'He must know that even

196

when the others at ANTIDOTE learn the truth about Sarah, they'll be loath to make it public.'

'But what did Marcus Pardela hope to achieve?' asked Nosh. 'Sarah could let him know when ANTIDOTE were organizing protest marches against them and such like, but that was it.'

'No, it's more than that,' I said slowly. 'ANTIDOTE march against other companies, not just Shelby's. If Sarah was just running things for Marcus Pardela then he could make sure they attacked his rivals more often than they did his company.'

'And he would get an instant list of all those people against his company,' Julian added. 'A list of ANTIDOTE supporters.'

We all fell silent, both impressed and appalled at the deviousness of Pardela's antics. Nosh pointed to the screen. 'When Sarah says that she doesn't think the person who's on to her "knows anything else" – what does she mean? What else is there to know?'

'That's a good question,' I considered.

'Isn't that irrelevant?' said Halle. 'Surely what we need to think about now is how to use this information.'

Silence.

'It's not enough.' Julian said at last. 'It's not

enough to force Pardela's hand. We need something more.'

'We don't have anything else.' Halle shook her head.

'We have the other floppy disk Halle brought home. There may be something on that?' I suggested.

'Can you print out all the information on it?' Julian asked.

'Yeah, but it'll run to hundreds of pages,' I said.

'We'll split all the pages between the four of us. That'll make the task a bit easier,' said Julian. 'We can each read through the pages and see if we can find anything we can use.'

I loaded up the other floppy and typed in the command to send all the files copied across that day to the printer.

'This is going to take some time,' I said.

'We're on to the mole but, thanks to Sarah's mail message, Marcus Pardela is also on to us. Each of us will have to go through our share of the printed-out pages, tonight.'

Nosh and I exchanged a glance. Nosh was right. It did feel like Julian was trying to take over. I suppose he thought that because he was the oldest he should be in charge. But I didn't say anything. Thanks to him we now knew who the mole was.

'Elliot, can you make me a copy of your

e-mail floppy?' Julian asked suddenly.

'Surely we don't need to read Rohan's mail messages,' I said. 'We know Sarah's the mole.'

'I don't want to load the floppy onto Rohan's machine. I had someone else's PC in mind.'

'Whose?' I asked.

'I won't say – in case I don't manage it,' Julian said mysteriously. 'But if I do pull it off, we'll have all the info we'll ever need to stop Pardela in his tracks.'

There was no mistaking the gleam of satisfaction on Julian's face at the thought of it.

'Now that we know who the mole is, do I have to go back to ANTIDOTE tomorrow?' Halle asked.

'I don't see why,' I said. 'Or maybe it would be better if you did go for a couple of days, in case Sarah gets suspicious.'

'At least I can have a lie-in. They don't need me until two o'clock tomorrow afternoon,' Halle said.

As I formatted and created a new e-mail floppy, Julian asked, 'Has anyone got any other suggestions?'

'There's still my mum's organizer,' I admitted. 'I'm sure there's something on that. Something more than just the identity of the ANTIDOTE mole. But I haven't managed to crack the password yet.'

'But are you certain it's got something on it that we can use?' asked Julian.

I shook my head.

'D'you think you'll be able to crack the password – and soon?' asked Julian.

All eyes were on me. I took a deep breath. 'By tomorrow at the latest,' I said.

And what's more I would do it, too. I had to. I just had to.

TUESDAY

18

Eureka!

My eyes were full of sand and poised precariously on two matchsticks. My whole head ached. Even my eyebrows were hurting. It was half past four in the morning and I hadn't had one wink of sleep yet. Nosh had checked through the listings I'd given him and fallen asleep over an hour ago. I'd finished checking my print-outs about an hour ago and I never wanted to go through that again. I would've had more fun watching my fingernails grow.

Since then, I'd been trying to work out Mum's password. And I have to admit, I was getting desperate. Maybe the eighteen letters in the password were the first eighteen letters of the alphabet? No. The last eighteen letters of the alphabet. Nope.

Without warning the bedroom door opened. It was Nosh's dad. It was hard to say which one of us was more surprised.

'Elliot? What on earth are you doing? You should've been asleep hours ago.'

'I . . . I . . .'

'Come on. Put down your toy. It'll still be there when you wake up,' said Nosh's dad. 'Besides, you won't be too cute if you don't get your beauty sleep, now will you?'

My face burning, I stretched up to switch off my bedside lamp, before scooting under the duvet.

'Good night, Elliot.'

'Good night.'

But the moment the light was off and the door closed, I sat bolt upright.

Eureka! I had it!

Switching on the bedside light again, I stared down at the organizer screen telling myself that it couldn't be that simple – could it? My fingers started to tremble as I tried yet another password:

ELLIOT YOU'RE CUTE

The screen cleared momentarily, then lots of different icons appeared. *I was in!*

'Yaahoo!' I shouted. I quickly bit my lip as I remembered what time it was.

'Whasamata?' Nosh asked sleepily.

'Nosh, wake up. I did it!' I told him, waving the organizer above my head.

He was instantly awake.

'You didn't.' Nosh was impressed. 'What was the password, then?'

'That doesn't matter,' I dismissed. I

certainly wasn't going to tell him that! 'The point is, we're in.'

'So what's on it?'

I sat down at the edge of my bed and started going through the various files Mum had on her organizer. Nosh came and sat beside me. There was a file called SHELBY in Mum's word processing directory, so I opened that one first.

At the very top of the file was a date, which was almost two and a half years in the past. As I looked at the rest of the file, I could've howled. It was gobbledy-gook! Pure and utter gibberish!

'What's all that, then?' Nosh asked.

'The file has been computer coded,' I replied. 'And there's no way I can decrypt the file without the original program.'

'Is that on the organizer too?' Nosh asked.

I checked but there was no file that even came close to doing that. I went back into the coded SHELBY file and scrolled down it, hoping against hope that the whole thing wouldn't be encrypted. It was. At the very end of the file was a name – Paul S. C. Darmare – but that was it. I checked every other file on Mum's organizer. She had a number of what she called 'case files' which were like something out of Sherlock Holmes. Like when such and such a person had entered a restaurant, or where another person kept their safe. They made Mum seem more like a private investigator than a secretary, but then I knew she wasn't a secretary. She'd told me so herself. I went through every other file on the system, including Mum's diary which was amazing in itself, but there was nothing else about Shelby's. Nosh could see how disappointed I was.

'The SHELBY file was copied onto this organizer on the same day that Mum . . . that Uncle Robert was arrested,' I said. 'Why would she want to download a file that's over two years old?' I stared at the hieroglyphics on the screen, willing them to change into English before my eyes.

'Come on, Elliot. We're both dog-tired. Let's get some sleep and maybe we'll be able to do more in the morning.'

I was about to argue but my body made the decision for me. I was shattered.

'OK!' I sighed.

And we each got into our beds. Within seconds I was out.

Halle scrutinized the SHELBY file on Mum's organizer. Her lips drooped with frustration. She glared at Nosh and me as if we were doing it deliberately.

'Is that it, then?'

I sighed. 'I'm afraid so.'

'Who's Paul S. C. Darmare?' Halle asked.

'No idea.'

'Does he work for Shelby's, then?'

'Haven't a clue,' I replied.

'That's a fat lot of use,' Halle said with disgust.

'Just because . . . I . . .' My voice drifted to a stop.

'What's the matter?' asked Nosh.

'Hang on. We're not beaten yet. There are all kinds of coding and decoding programs on the Internet. Why don't I try one of those?' I said.

'Will that work?' Halle said, surprised.

'We won't know until we try it,' I said.

'What're we waiting for?' Halle grinned. 'I've got a good feeling about this.'

Minutes later, we were in front of Mum's PC and had logged on to her Internet account. I did a search for any programs which encrypted and decrypted data files. A screenful of file names and locations appeared. As I printed off the list, I had another brainwave.

'I'm really on form this morning! I must go without sleep more often,' I grinned. 'I've had an idea. Why don't we check out the world-wide web page for Shelby's?'

'Check out the what?' Nosh asked.

'Lots of companies are on the Internet now. They give company details, advertise their services, show some of their most important staff – all that sort of stuff,' I explained. 'We might find Paul Darmare mentioned.'

'Don't forget his middle initials,' said Halle.

I started searching for a Shelby's page. More good luck was coming my way. Shelby and Pardela Pharmaceuticals were on the Internet. I scanned the screen but there was no mention of a Paul Darmare.

'I'll try calling up more information about Marcus Pardela,' I said.

Using the mouse to click on Pardela's name, we waited impatiently as several seconds later, three pages were downloaded. The moment I clicked on the first page, a video of Marcus Pardela's smiling face started chatting on about how wonderful his company was. How they cared about people and the environment as any responsible company would. I almost puked! Clicking on his face to shut him up, I then turned to the information all around the box that had his video image in it. It was like reading his CV. It talked about his qualifications, the schools he'd been to, and gave a lot of boring detail about how he and Joshua Shelby first started up the company almost twenty-five years before. At the end of the third page were some of his family details.

'He's got his priorities right,' Halle said with disgust. 'He talks about his family last.'

Nosh was the one who spotted it first.

'Look at that!' he said, quietly.

There, at the bottom of the screen, was a sentence that said:

Marcus Pardela is divorced with three children, Paul, Chandla and Julian.

'Julian . . .' Nosh said, stunned.

'My Julian's surname is Dulles, you trouble-stirring little weasel.' Halle glared at Nosh.

'Come off it, Nosh! It can't be the same guy,' I scoffed.

'Click on their names. Let's see what comes up,' said Nosh.

I did as he suggested just to humour him. Moments later, what was obviously a family photograph appeared on the screen. A girl with dark hair, stood between two boys. From the look of it, the photo was about three or four years old, but there was no doubt about it. It was the same Julian. Halle's boyfriend was Marcus Pardela's son.

Halle looked as if she'd just been slapped.

'I don't believe it . . .' she whispered.

'It's right there – in full colour,' Nosh said furiously. 'Your boyfriend is Pardela's son. He's probably been reporting everything we've said and done straight back to his dad.'

'He wouldn't do that.' Halle's eyes took on a steely glint. 'Julian wouldn't do that. I met him on an ANTIDOTE march, for goodness' sake.'

As for me – it was as if every hope, every optimistic thought I'd allowed myself, had just been totally wiped out.

'Halle, if you didn't want to help me, you should've just said so,' I hissed at her. 'You shouldn't have set me up like that.'

'I didn't set you up. I swear I didn't,' Halle denied.

'You must have known Julian's surname – or couldn't you put two and two together?' I fumed.

'Listen here, Elliot. Julian told me his surname was Dulles. He never said one word about being Marcus Pardela's son.'

'He and his dad must've had a real good laugh at us when he left last night.' To my embarrassment, my eyes began to sting. I actually wanted to cry, which of course made me even madder at Halle. 'How could you, Halle?'

'You're not listening to me!' Halle shouted. 'I didn't know. Look, there must be some mistake.'

She pushed me to one side and moved in for a closer look at the screen.

'There's no mistake,' Nosh said. 'Anyone with half an eye could see it's your boyfriend.'

The insistent peal of the doorbell was like cold water thrown over all of us.

Giving Halle a lasering look, Nosh headed downstairs. I was dishing out some nasty looks of my own. Not that Halle caught many of them. She was too busy staring in disbelief at the screen.

If seeing Julian on the screen was a shock, seeing him in person was an even bigger one. He stepped through the door and his querying expression turned into a frown.

'What's wrong?' he asked.

Halle stood up and regarded him without saying a word.

'Oh! You know,' Julian said, quietly.

'So it's true.' Halle's voice gave an odd hic.

'It's true that I'm Marcus Pardela's son. But that's the only thing that's true. Until last night, I hadn't seen him in over three months.'

'You saw him last night?' Nosh asked.

Julian nodded.

'Why?' said Nosh belligerently.

'I wanted to help Elliot and his family – so I went to my father's flat, hoping I could copy his mail messages onto the floppy Elliot gave me,' Julian explained. He dug into his jacket pocket and brought out the floppy. 'Here you are, Elliot. I don't know what's on it but I hope it's something you can use.'

'Are we supposed to believe that?' Nosh scoffed.

'Yes, because it's true.' Julian's voice raised just a fraction.

'You said your name was Julian Dulles,' said Halle.

'It is. I started using my mother's maiden name over four years ago when Mum and Dad got divorced.'

'So when we first told you about Elliot's mum and Shelby's Pharmaceuticals, why didn't you tell us who you really were then?' Halle accused.

'Because I really am Julian Dulles. Look, what is this? You've all decided that I'm guilty without even hearing my side of it.'

'What did you tell your dad about Mum and Uncle Robert and me?' I had to ask, although I couldn't trust myself to speak without blubbing.

'Nothing. Absolutely nothing. He doesn't even know that I know you,' Julian said earnestly. 'Dad was in a rage because he'd just read Sarah Irving's mail message and he knew the cat was out of the bag.'

'I don't believe you,' said Nosh.

Halle and I didn't say a word. We didn't have to. Julian knew how we felt from our expressions. He lowered his head briefly and when he straightened up again, his eyes were bitter like a long, hard winter.

'All my life I've been judged by what my father is and does and says. Is it any wonder I changed my name? And you, Halle, after all the time we've been together, I would've thought you'd know me better than that.'

Still no-one spoke.

'Thanks a lot – all of you.' Julian placed the floppy disk on the PC table and after one last bitter glance, he left the room.

19

The Real Deal

'Excuse me,' Halle said quietly.

As she headed out of the room, Nosh said, 'He's not worth it, Halle. He . . .'

'Shut up, Nosh. Just shut up.' Halle rounded on him.

It wasn't so much her words as the tears running down her face that finally made Nosh keep quiet. Halle all but sprinted from the room. Moments later, the front door was slammed shut.

'Nosh, I . . . if you don't mind, I think I'd like to spend some time on my own,' I told him.

'It's not my fault . . .'

'I never said it was,' I replied impatiently. 'The whole world doesn't revolve around you, you know.'

Nosh looked at me, then turned and left the room. Again, the front door was slammed shut. The moment I knew I was alone, I buried my head in my hands as I tried to collect my thoughts. Exactly how much had Julian been told, how much did he know about this whole business? I tried to gauge just how much he'd hurt us.

It was my fault. I should never have involved so many people in this. Taking a deep breath, then another, I sat back in my chair. It was no good beating myself up about it. I had to decide what to do next to help Mum. If I could do that then the last few days wouldn't have been a total waste. I sensed the key to all this was the coded file on Mum's organizer. I loaded the SHELBY file back up onto the PC and started copying down the decoding programs that were scattered across the Internet. The telephone bill would be horrendous but I figured that if it helped Mum, then she wouldn't mind *too* much.

When I'd downloaded all of the coding/ decoding programs onto the hard disk, I got to work. It was a long, slow, laborious process. I had to run each program, specifying the input file as the SHELBY file I'd copied from the organizer. The first seven programs just made the SHELBY file worse or crashed out, unable to decode it.

Programs eight, nine and ten must've been put on the Internet for a joke. They were useless. I could've written better decoders than that in one minute flat. Then I tried the eleventh program. In about two seconds flat, the screen said:

FILE DECODED: ANOTHER?

I typed in 'N' for no, then typed the new decoded output file. As the data came up on the screen, I sat back, intensely frustrated. The coded gibberish made more sense! This new decoded file was the last page of a report of some kind that was something to do with accounting but I couldn't make head nor tail of it. The title of the report – PROJECTED EXPENDITURE – was about the only bit that didn't immediately whizz over my head. There had to be something to this file – something that made Shelby's desperate to get my mum and uncle out of the picture. I leaned forward for a closer look. One bit of the report showed what the rent per year would be at a particular address. The address rang all kinds of bells in my head. Slowly, I realized why.

It was the address of the ANTIDOTE office.

This was obviously a report written by someone when ANTIDOTE was first started up. At the bottom of the report, just above Paul Darmare's name was the line:

PROJECT APPROVED: BUDGET APPROVED.

The rest of the file had things in it like future staff salaries and the cost of office equipment, etc. Was this really the file that so many people were trying to get their hands on? Why? I looked at the name at the bottom of the report. Paul S. C. Darmare. I went downstairs and phoned the ANTIDOTE office.

'Hi. Can I speak to Paul Darmare, please?' I asked in my best grown-up voice.

'Who?' The woman's voice at the other end of the phone asked. It sounded like Sarah Irving. I had to really resist the temptation to accuse her over the phone.

'Paul Darmare,' I repeated, stonily.

'We don't have anyone here by that name,' Sarah said.

'How long ago did he leave your company, then?' I said.

'We've never had a Paul Darmare working here. Who is this?'

'But Paul Darmare is the one who set up your organization,' I said, confused.

'No, we received our major funding from an anonymous source,' said Sarah. '*Who is this?*'

'It doesn't matter. Sorry to bother you. Bye.' I put the phone down before the woman could ask me any more questions.

So who was Paul Darmare?

I trudged back upstairs, deep in thought. Paul S. C. Darmare . . . Every time I sorted out one problem, two more popped up in its place.

'Come on, Elliot!' I muttered. 'Think!'

Once I was in front of the PC again, I saw the disk Julian had left behind. Should I risk it? It could be a booby trap and wipe out every piece of information on Mum's hard disk . . . I picked up the floppy, turning it over and over in my hands. Maybe we had been unfair . . . ? But it was such a shock. And suppose the disk contained his dad's mail messages, just as Julian had said.

I stuck the floppy in its drive before I could change my mind. Searching through the floppy disk, I found only mail message directories. Holding my breath, I went for it. I copied all the data from the floppy up to the hard disk. Then I specified the new directory containing Marcus Pardela's mail messages as my own mail message account. It worked just as it had before. Each mail message account was controlled by a user identification and a password, but these could be set up so that you didn't have to type them in each time. As long as all the mail message directories or areas were copied across onto the floppy, then I had no problem getting into other people's mail messages. It meant that although I couldn't change any of Marcus Pardela's details, I could read his messages.

And he had hundreds. I displayed the list of all his mail messages sent out over the last month and it literally ran into the hundreds. I called up some likely-looking ones and it was all finance or snotty instructions to people I didn't know. But then I hit upon something strange.

One of the messages I retrieved didn't have Marcus Pardela's name at the bottom of it as all the others did. Instead it said, PAUL S.C. DARMARE.

So Marcus Pardela knew this mystery man. But I was still in the dark. Why was Paul Darmare using Marcus Pardela's account to send messages when he could just as easily set up his own account? I entered the command to display only those mail messages that had Paul Darmare's name in them somewhere. There were quite a few. Most of them were to do with financial stuff, but a number of them were sarcastic memos sent out to slag off the recipient. Paul Darmare was obviously just as charming as Marcus Pardela . . .

And then it hit me – like a bolt of lightning. It couldn't be . . . It just couldn't be . . .

Writing Paul S.C. Darmare's name down on a piece of paper, I then rearranged the letters. I was right. The evidence was in front of me and yet I still found it hard to believe I was right. If you rearranged the letters of Paul S.C. Darmare you got . . . Marcus Pardela.

There was no doubt about it. I went back to

the SHELBY file I'd copied up from Mum's organizer. No doubt about it.

ANTIDOTE had been set up and funded by *Marcus Pardela*.

But why? I couldn't believe Marcus Pardela set up ANTIDOTE out of the goodness of his heart, so why? Unless . . . unless it was to make sure that he always had total control of ANTIDOTE. Having a mole at their offices obviously wasn't enough. If he owned the entire organization, he could set them on his rivals whenever he wanted to. And it would also provide him with a good way of finding out exactly who his opponents were.

I sat back, as the full implications of what he'd done hit me. Is that what he'd meant in his original memo when he told Joshua Shelby to remember 'just whose idea all this was in the first place'? At last it all made sense. The march against Shelby's over the weekend had just been – what do they call it? – window dressing. And he'd managed to make ANTIDOTE look bad because of the fire at Shelby's. But now I thought about it, ANTIDOTE were a lot more active in pursuing other chemical and pharmaceutical companies.

Did that mean that more people than Sarah Irving were reporting back to Marcus Pardela? I couldn't believe that all those people at ANTIDOTE would work there, knowing that their wages, their funding, everything they were was a direct result of Marcus Pardela's scheming.

The phone had rung a few times before I realized it. I bounded down the stairs and picked it up.

'Hello?'

'Elliot? Thank God you're OK.'

'Mum! Mum, I've figured it out from your organizer,' I burst out. 'ANTIDOTE was set up by Marcus Pardela. That's what he and that other guy, Joshua Shelby, are so desperate to keep hidden. That's the real deal, I'm sure of it.'

'Elliot . . .'

'I managed to decode the file on your organizer. It was signed by someone called Paul S. C. Darmare, but that's just an anagram for Marcus Pardela,' I rushed on. 'Is that why they set up you and Uncle Robert? Because they didn't want you decoding the SHELBY file and making the information public?'

Click . . .

Only then did I remember what Mum had said about our phone being bugged. I stared at the receiver, horrified. I could've bitten my tongue off. How could I be so *stupid*!

'Mum, I'm sorry . . .'

'Elliot, listen to me very carefully,' Mum said. There was no trace of a smile in her voice. She sounded . . . she was frightened and for the first time she made no attempt to hide it. 'I want you to reformat my hard disk to wipe out everything on it. Then I want you to reset my organizer to wipe out everything on that. Then you're to leave the house and never enter it again, until I get back. Is that understood?'

'But Mum . . .'

'IS THAT UNDERSTOOD?' Mum shouted at me.

Click . . .

'Yes, Mum.'

'You're to leave that house and not say a word about what you found out to anyone. Do you promise me?'

'Yes, Mum, but I . . .'

'Elliot, do as I tell you right now. There's no time to waste.'

'OK, but . . .'

'Elliot, I . . .'

There was a muffled sound, followed by a bang as if the receiver had been dropped. It sounded like thunder in my ear.

'Mum? Mum?'

There was no answer.

'Mum?' I tried again.

It wasn't as if the phone had been replaced.

There was no dialling tone, just an eerie silence.

I hung up, wondering what had happened. Mum must've seen something and had to make a run for it. But Pardela's lot would never catch up with my mum. She was too smart for them. Still, if Mum wanted me to delete all the data on her hard disk, that's what I'd do. But she hadn't said anything about printing out a few details first.

WEDNESDAY

20

The Letter

As I ate my breakfast on Wednesday morning, it was as if the whole weight of the world had been lifted from my shoulders. I was still kicking myself for blurting everything out over the phone, but at least Marcus Pardela knew that Mum and I were on to him. Now Mum had some ammunition to make him confess the truth – that Mum didn't break into his building. He'd have to confess that he got someone to set up Mum and Uncle Robert, and our lives could go back to what they were. But looking around the breakfast table, I was the only one who didn't have a face like a handful of mince – as Nosh would say.

Halle's eyes were red and Nosh was concentrating on his breakfast without looking at me.

'Halle, Julian's OK. That floppy disk *did* contain his dad's mail messages. I think everything he said was true,' I told her.

She looked up, frowning. 'You believe him.'

'Yeah. After all, he didn't have to help me,' I replied.

'He should have told me the truth.'

'But I can see why he didn't,' I said carefully.

Nosh's dad watched us, his ears and eyes peeled. 'Have you broken up with your boyfriend, then?' he asked.

'I don't know,' Halle replied.

'There's something more going on here. Would someone like to bring me up to date?' Nosh's dad asked hopefully.

'No!' Halle, Nosh and I all spoke in unison. It broke the ice. We glanced around the table and started laughing.

'Hhmm!' Nosh's dad returned to his toast, still keeping his eyes on us.

'Elliot, you've got a letter.' Nosh's mum entered the kitchen, surprise in her voice. 'It was sent here. No . . . Hang on, it hasn't got a stamp on it. It must've been hand delivered.'

She handed it over and I tore the envelope open. It had to be from Mum, giving me further instructions. It wasn't.

Dear Elliot,
How are you? We thought you'd be pleased to know that your mother is with us. She's perfectly safe and looking forward to seeing you again. Be ready to be picked up by car

at nine o'clock tonight, so you can be with her. Everything has been arranged. Don't be alarmed but your mother is a bit under the weather. Nothing too serious, she's just desperate to see you again. As close as you two are, I'm sure you realize that her health and happiness all depend on you. She'd rather you told no-one the contents of this letter. As far as this whole Shelby business is concerned, we're <u>still</u> watching and listening – to ensure the safety of everyone concerned. Don't worry about a thing – we're <u>everywhere</u>.

Also, your mother would like you to bring her organizer and all the print-outs you made yesterday. I'm sure you won't mind doing that. It's what your mother wants. I look forward to seeing you again later, but not as much as your mother does.

Steve

And there, stuck to the bottom of the letter was the locket I'd bought Mum for her birthday last year. She never, ever took it off.

So it was true. They did have her.

My head was spinning. My stomach was heaving about like clothes in a washing-machine. I read the letter again, and then a third time. I unstuck the locket and gripped it in my fist.

'Elliot, are you OK?' Nosh asked.

I looked up, but I'd barely heard Nosh. The whole kitchen was swimming around my head.

'Elliot, what's wrong?' Nosh's mum asked. 'Was that letter bad news?'

I looked down at the letter in my hand, still in a daze. Nosh's mum walked around the breakfast table to read the letter over my shoulder. Only then did I break out of my stupor. I crumpled up the letter and stuffed it in my pocket.

Nosh's mum veered off to the fridge to get some more milk. I knew I'd been rude – especially after all she'd done for me – but . . . but they had Mum. I suddenly felt so sick. What on earth could they hope to achieve? If they listened in on my conversation with Mum – and they obviously had – then they must know that Mum told me to keep my mouth shut, and I'd done exactly that.

The print-outs . . .

The letter said I should bring the print-outs. How had they known I'd made any in the first place? Unless more than the phone was bugged in our house? Was that possible? I gritted my teeth. I should've thought of that before. If that was the case, then they'd been on to us every step of the way. Maybe they didn't expect me to get this far?

Maybe they didn't expect that I'd find out the truth about ANTIDOTE? But all that was beside the point now. They had Mum. And at nine o'clock tonight, they'd have me as well.

I had to do something. *Had to*. But what? My mind was a blank. I was desperate. What could I do. Think! *Think!*

I looked around the kitchen frantically, hoping, I suppose, that some idea would leap out at me from behind the hob or something. Only then did I realize that every eye was on me. I lowered my gaze at once and carried on with my breakfast.

'Elliot . . .' Nosh's dad began, uncertainly. 'You do know that if you're in trouble, any kind of trouble, we'd all help out, in any way we could.'

'Thanks,' I mumbled. 'It's just that . . . just that, Mum's sending someone to pick me up at nine o'clock tonight.'

It was the only thing I could think of. I had to give them a reason why I needed to leave the house later without being asked too many questions.

'That letter was from your mum?' Nosh's eyes were wide.

'No, it was from a . . . friend of hers. She's sending a car to pick me up later. She wants us to be together,' I explained.

'Elliot, I'm not sure that's such a good idea . . .' Nosh's mum began.

'I want to be with my mum,' I interrupted. 'Please don't try and stop me. We will be back. It's not for ever.'

Only, as I said it, I realized that that's exactly what it might be. If I didn't come up with something – fast – Mum and I would disappear for ever.

'Let me see the letter,' Nosh's mum ordered.

My hand flew protectively to the outside of my pocket.

'Elliot, I'm not letting you go anywhere until I see that letter,' said Nosh's mum.

Reluctantly, I dug out the letter and read it again myself – even though every word was burned into my brain. It was a clever letter, very clever indeed. It was full of threats and hidden meanings but anyone reading it without knowing what was going on, would take it for what it seemed – perfectly harmless. I handed it over to Nosh's mum. I stared at her as she read, willing her to go beyond the words and realize the menace of the letter, willing her to read my mind and know just how terrified I really was. After a few moments, Nosh's mum passed it back.

'Who's Steve?' Nosh's mum questioned.

'A friend of Mum's,' I replied instantly. 'Nosh has met him.'

Nosh stared when I said that.

'Remember? The guy with the pony-tail who told us about my uncle?' I said carefully. I had no idea if I was right, but I suspected that I was.

'Oh – *him* . . .' Nosh said. 'Yeah, I've met him all right.'

'From your voice, I take it you didn't like him much,' Nosh's dad smiled.

'Not much.' Nosh regarded the letter in my hand. Quickly I crumpled it and put it in my pocket again. I didn't want anyone else asking to read it – especially not Nosh. He'd know what it meant straight away. I needn't have worried. Nosh bowed his head and concentrated on his breakfast. I don't know if I was glad or disappointed. Maybe a little of both.

'OK, Elliot. I guess that's all right, then,' Nosh's mum said doubtfully. She frowned at her husband but said nothing else.

I slumped in my chair. If only there was someone I could safely confide in. If only there was someone I could tell.

And that's when it occurred to me that there was someone – or rather, something – I could tell. I'd dictate the whole thing into Mum's PC and give Nosh the disks. Marcus Pardela wouldn't have things all his own way.

Marcus Pardela. I hated him so much, it scared me. I'd never even met the man, only seen him on telly. And yet he had the power to rule over our lives, to turn them upside down. To try and get rid of us like so much rubbish. I wouldn't let him get away with it. I wouldn't.

So that's it, Nosh. The whole story. In case you're wondering, that's a CD I've got playing in the background. It was to stop Pardela and his lot from eavesdropping on me, just in case there is a bug in this room. All they'd pick up is Michael Jackson's voice, but the PC picked up mine.

So, as I said at the beginning, Nosh, if I'm not back tomorrow, take these disks to the police. Don't let Pardela get away with it. I'm counting on you. Don't let me down.

NOW

21

The Encounter

I sat in the back of the car, looking out of the window. The guy with the pony-tail who'd chased Mum sat beside me. There was no getting away from the satisfied smirk on his face. He thought his side had won. Well, maybe they'd won the battle but they wouldn't win the war. I turned back to the car window, drinking in every sight, every sound we passed – as if I was experiencing them for the first time. As if I'd never experience them again. The darkness, the street lights, the people, the shops . . . they were all precious.

The minutes dragged into hours and still we kept driving – until, at last, the car turned down a driveway and stopped outside a large farmhouse, with what looked like a barn next to it. I could only see that much because of the light coming from the farmhouse itself. I looked up. There were no stars. It must've been too cloudy, but it was too dark to even see the clouds. I'd never seen darkness like it.

It was as if the whole world except for the two buildings before me had been swallowed up. Or maybe we were the ones who'd fallen off the edge of the world.

The driver leapt out of the car, then opened my door. He didn't wait for me to step out. He dragged me out.

'Watch it,' I hissed at him.

Smiler grinned maliciously at me and took over the grip on my arm, digging his fingers into my flesh. With a spiteful yank, he pulled me towards the house. The front door opened even before we got there – and I got my first sight of Marcus Pardela, in the flesh. He was taller than I'd expected, taller and thinner. Smiler pushed me past him and into one of the rooms on the ground floor. It was huge and covered in floor-to-ceiling shelves, each crammed with books.

'Thanks, Steve. Wait outside until I call you,' Marcus commanded.

So I was right. He was Steve. I wondered why he bothered to use his real name in the letter he left for me. But then, why not? He didn't leave his surname, so there was no way to trace him.

'Elliot!'

'Mum!'

Only then did Smiler let me go. I flew to Mum and we hugged each other, tight, tight.

She looked so tired and unhappy. Smiler left the room, without saying a word.

'You don't need to do this, Pardela. Let my son go,' Mum said over my head.

'He knows as much, if not more than you do,' Marcus Pardela replied. 'How can I let him go?'

'I don't care about you or your business,' I shouted at him. 'I just wanted to do something to help Mum.'

'You should've worried less about her and more about yourself,' Marcus told me.

'What're you going to do with us?' Mum asked softly.

'Elliot, give me the print-outs you made yesterday,' Marcus demanded.

He walked over to me, his hand outstretched. I would've liked to spit in his eye, if I could reach it, but reluctantly I did as he asked.

'Are these the only copies?'

I nodded.

'And your mum's organizer, if you don't mind,' Marcus smarmed.

'I do mind,' I told him. But I handed that over as well.

Someone else moved out of the shadows in one corner of the room. I hadn't even realized that there was someone there until he walked towards us.

'Marcus, I don't like this . . .'

'Ian Macmillan!' I said, aghast.

'Marcus,' Ian frowned, 'I want to be well away from this place, before . . . before . . .'

'Say it,' Mum ordered. 'Before he gets rid of my son and me. Before we disappear. Before he *kills* us. Because that's what he's going to do. Oh, he won't do it personally – he wouldn't get his own hands dirty, but he'll have it done. That's the kind of man you're working for, Ian.'

'Shut up, Lisa,' Ian shouted. 'If you'd stayed out of this . . .'

'Then someone else would be standing here instead of me and my son,' Mum interrupted. 'The faces would've been different, but what Marcus is about to do would've been exactly the same.'

'Shut up! SHUT UP!' Ian practically screamed at her.

'Calm down, Ian. Can't you tell she's just trying to bait you?' Marcus soothed.

Ian glared at Mum, but said nothing.

'So you're working for Pardela as well as Sarah,' I realized.

'Sarah doesn't work for him. Sarah doesn't know anything about Marcus Pardela,' Ian snorted.

'But the mail message . . .'

'I sent it from her PC. It's called covering your tracks.'

So we'd got that completely wrong. I glanced up at Mum who was still hugging me. I'd never been so frightened in my life, but strangely enough, part of me felt calm and almost happy now that I was back with Mum. I just wished it was under different circumstances

'And now I think it's time for you two to visit my barn,' Marcus smiled silkily.

Mum's arms tightened around me fractionally. I could feel her body, tense and stiff with nerves.

'I don't want to see it, thanks,' Mum said lightly. 'Once you've seen one barn, you've seen them all.'

'I'm sorry about this, Lisa – I really am. But like you and Elliot, I too have run out of choices,' said Marcus.

And in that moment, I knew that this was all horribly real and Marcus was going to do it. He was going to kill us . . .

Then the doorbell rang.

'Go and see who that is,' Marcus demanded of Ian.

The moment he was out of the room, Marcus sat down and watched us. Mum pushed me behind her and stood stock still.

'I'm not going to let you hurt my son,' Mum said, softly.

'I wish there was some other way. I really do,' Marcus shrugged.

There was a sudden commotion outside the room, then the door burst open.

'Julian!' Marcus Pardela sprang out of his chair. 'What're you doing here?'

Julian looked around the room, then directly at Mum and me. For a split second I thought he was there to back up his dad, that he was part of the team with his dad. Until, that is, Julian turned to face him.

'Halle and Nosh phoned me and told me that something was wrong. I know your methods, Dad – so when Steve came to pick up Elliot, I followed them,' Julian said, loathing dripping from every word.

'You have no business here,' Marcus Pardela raged. 'Get in your car and drive away – now.'

'No, Dad.' Julian dug his hands into his pockets, then took them out again. 'No, I won't. I'm going to stand up to you. It's about time.'

'Julian . . .'

'You're despicable,' Julian hissed. 'You don't care about anyone or anything but money. All you want to do is make more and more and more. When will you make enough,

Dad? You're a millionaire now. How much is enough?'

'Don't talk to me like that, boy. You'll talk to me with respect or not at all.'

'Respect has to be earned. You never did understand that,' Julian said bitterly. 'But understand this, anything you do to Elliot and his mum, you'll have to do to me as well.'

'Don't be ridiculous,' Marcus dismissed.

'I mean it. I'm not leaving, and I'm not going to let you harm them.' Julian walked over to stand by us.

I smiled up at him. How could I have called this man a Cedric! He was brill!

'Julian, you don't know what you're getting yourself into,' Marcus said. 'Leave now and we'll say no more about it.'

'I can't do that, Dad. And besides, I didn't come alone.'

As the door opened, Marcus Pardela's eyes weren't the only ones to bulge out. Halle, Nosh, Nosh's mum and dad, Sarah Irving and Rohan Adjava stood in the doorway. I couldn't see the driver of the car that'd brought me to this farmhouse, but Smiler was being held by Rohan and Nosh's dad. He struggled violently, kicking out and cursing as if his life depended on it.

'What the . . . ?'

'Are you ready to take on all of us, Dad?

Because that's what you're going to have to do,' Julian told him.

Marcus looked around. I could see the wheels at work in his head. It was like watching evil personified.

'Let . . . me . . . go . . .' Smiler kicked out even more than before.

Nosh's dad released Smiler momentarily to get a better grip on him, but that was all Smiler needed. He drew back his elbow and smashed Rohan in the ribs. Rohan immediately doubled over, coughing for breath. Smiler reached into his inside jacket pocket, but before anyone else could say or do a thing, Halle was before him. And moments later, Smiler was flat on his back and out for the count. Halle glared down at him as she shook her hand and rubbed her knuckles.

'Lucky for you I hate violence!' Halle told Smiler's prostrate body. 'Or you'd be in real trouble.'

'Yes! Way to go, Halle!' Nosh looked at his sister with something suspiciously like hero worship in his eyes.

'Look, I think there's been a misunderstanding here. You're all free to go.' Marcus turned to Mum and me. '*All* of you. But it's in no-one's best interests to make this public. I have a lot of friends who could make life . . . shall we say, very sticky, for each and every one of you. And you people from ANTI-DOTE, you stand to lose as much as I do if the truth comes out.'

Sarah Irving stepped into the room. 'ANTI-DOTE is a good organization. I'm not going to let you bury us. We might have to change offices, even change our name, but we'll survive. And as for you, Ian, don't bother coming to work tomorrow.'

'Marcus . . .' Ian appealed directly to his boss.

'Dad, you've lost. For the first time in your life, you've lost,' Julian smiled sadly. 'Something tells me it won't be the last time either. We should make all this public but we'll make a deal with you. You tell the police that the video tape showing Elliot's mum and uncle breaking into your building is a fake, and we might consider keeping all this quiet.'

'How am I meant to explain away a tape showing their faces?' Marcus frowned.

'You're an ace businessman. You'll think of something,' Julian dismissed. 'After all, you wouldn't like it to become public knowledge just exactly how you do business.'

'Julian, you should be on my side. You're still my son. I'm only doing this for you . . .'

'Don't give me that! You love yourself, no-one else. You never have done. You never will do. I can't bear even to be in the same room as you. You make me sick.' Julian spoke with such rage and hurt, that the room almost vibrated with it. 'You're going to make sure that the police know Elliot's mum and uncle were set up by you and your cronies. Understood?'

Marcus didn't answer. He didn't have to. I could well believe that it was the first time in his life he'd ever been dictated to. Julian escorted Mum and me out of the room. At the door he paused, then turned back to his father.

'Oh, and in case you were thinking of changing your mind about telling the police the truth . . .' Julian took a small voice-activated tape recorder out of his jacket pocket and held it up. The tape was still running. 'I hope I make myself clear.'

And with that, Julian left the room, closing the door quietly behind him. We all left the house shrouded in a strange silence. I think everyone was thinking about what might have happened to Mum and me . . . I know I was. Once we were outside the farmhouse, Julian seemed to slump.

'Are you OK?' Mum asked him at once.

He tried to smile, but couldn't quite manage it. 'I've been better,' he said at last.

'We're not really going to let your dad get away with it, are we?' Halle asked. 'I mean, I know he's your dad and all, but . . .'

'Once Elliot's mum and uncle are off the hook, then all deals are off,' Julian smiled, his eyes narrowed. For the first time, he reminded me of his father.

'You'd do that?' I asked him. 'You'd let the world know what your dad's really like?'

'Watch me!' Julian replied icily. 'My father's going to learn that he can't win – not all the time. Not if I have anything to do with it. I suspect that barn of his has a few secrets that are about ready to be shared, as well.'

I looked across at the barn and shivered. My imagination was working overtime now but something told me that the gruesome pictures in my head weren't too far off the mark.

'Mrs Gaines, can I give you a lift back to town?' Julian asked.

Mum smiled and nodded.

'I'll come with you too, if you like,' Halle told Julian.

'No, Halle. I think we've all had quite enough excitement for one night. You can come in our car,' her dad insisted.

'Oh, but . . .'

'Halle, can I come round to see you tomorrow?' Julian asked.

'I'd like that,' Halle smiled.

I watched as Nosh and his family got into their car. Rohan and Sarah got into theirs.

They'd all come to help Mum and me. It was hard to believe and yet here they were. I'd have to get the full story from Nosh as soon as I could. But right now, all I wanted to do was be with Mum.

'If you don't mind, Julian, can we get going, please? I don't want to stay around here for a moment longer than necessary,' Mum said. 'All I want to do now is go home.'

Mum and I sat in the back of Julian's car. Mum put her arm around my shoulder and for once I didn't shrug away and yell at her for showing me up. When we were on our way, Mum turned to me and said, 'You've certainly been busy.'

'You always said I could do anything if I just put my mind to it,' I reminded her.

'So I did.' Mum smiled. 'So I did.'

'And what about Uncle Robert? Will the police really let him go now?' I asked anxiously.

'Of course they will,' Mum reassured me.

'When?'

'Just as soon as Dad tells the police that your mum and uncle were both set up – on his orders,' Julian chipped in.

'So, with what we have on Marcus Pardela, my guess is your uncle will be out some time tomorrow afternoon,' Mum added.

I sagged back against her and felt myself

relax for the first time since I'd received the letter that same morning. My worst fears hadn't been realized. If anyone had asked me, I would never have guessed that we'd be driving home now – and with Julian of all people at the wheel.

'So you managed to use your uncle's disks?' Mum smiled at me.

At my totally blank look, she continued, 'You managed to work out how to use the disks your uncle left you?'

'I haven't even had them in the same room as our PC since he gave them to me,' I frowned.

'Then how did you figure out what was going on?' Mum asked.

'With Nosh and Halle's help,' I said. 'It's a long story.'

'And you didn't use your uncle's disks?'

'No. Why would I?' I asked, confused. 'I was rather busy trying to get you and Uncle out of trouble. I didn't have time to play games.'

'Games! Those three disks your uncle passed you contained the private mail messages of Rohan, Ian and Sarah. Your uncle was hoping you could use the disks to find out which one of them was betraying ANTIDOTE to Marcus Pardela.'

I stared at her. 'You're joking! You mean

I had their mail messages all this time . . .'

Julian began to laugh. I didn't see what was so funny.

'Hang on! Why didn't Uncle just go through their mail messages for himself?' I asked Mum.

'Your uncle managed to copy the mail messages of Rohan, Ian and Sarah while each of them was logged on to their message account but away from their PC. The only trouble was, once he'd copied their messages, he couldn't read them because he didn't have their e-mail passwords to get at them again. He reckoned that if anyone could crack their passwords, you could,' Mum explained.

'Why didn't he just tell me that?' I said.

'Your uncle didn't want to put any pressure on you,' Mum smiled.

'Why didn't Uncle copy each of their e-mail directories instead of just their messages. Then he wouldn't have needed their passwords,' I frowned.

'Can you do that? Would that work?' Mum asked doubtfully.

'That's what we ended up doing,' I told her, unable to resist a slight preen. 'If you copy someone's Internet and e-mail directories, then that person's user ID and password get copied too. You can't change their password because it's shown as hash signs or asterisks, but it doesn't stop you logging on to the Internet as them, and it certainly doesn't stop you using their e-mail system.'

'That's not terribly secure.' Mum wasn't impressed.

'Thank goodness! Or I'd never have got on the right track – even if we did think it was Sarah and not Ian,' I replied. 'Besides, it is secure as long as no-one has access to your PC.'

'Hhmm!'

I don't think Mum was totally convinced.

'So why did Uncle Robert say that the object of the game was to find out what the game was called?' I remembered.

'It was just a little joke of his.' Mum shrugged. 'He knew one of his colleagues was a traitor. He said that's what life is like and you should learn that sooner rather than later.'

'So the name of the game was "life",' I said. That sounded just like my uncle at his most cynical. But he didn't have it completely right. Yes, you did get people like Marcus Pardela and Ian, but you also had heroes like my mum and Julian, and good friends like Nosh and his family. My mind turned to the disks . . . I still couldn't get over it. After everything Nosh, Halle, Julian and I had been through! I could've solved the whole thing without leaving the house!

We travelled along in a companionable silence for a while. I caught Julian looking at Mum and me in his rear-view mirror a few times. He still looked upset.

'Mrs Gaines, I . . . I had a reason for wanting to drive you home,' Julian admitted. 'I . . . I want to apologize for what you've been through. I know my apology isn't much but . . .'

'Julian, it's not up to you to apologize for your father,' Mum said gently.

'No?' Julian's voice was bitter. 'That's not how I feel. I've been apologizing for him all my life. Saying sorry for his greed, sorry for his selfishness, sorry because I'm his son. Sorry, sorry, sorry.'

'Then stop, Julian. Just stop. Or you'll wake up one day and you won't know where he ends and you begin,' said Mum.

I wasn't sure but I thought I knew what Mum meant.

'Julian, I don't blame you at all – believe me. From what I've seen and heard so far, I should thank you instead. I don't think it's too dramatic to say, you probably saved our lives.'

''Course I didn't!' Julian actually sounded embarrassed.

'Yes, you did,' Mum smiled. She turned to me. 'And you, young man! When we get home I want to hear all about it. I can't imagine how you even began all this.'

'That's easy. I knew you didn't break into the Shelby building, so I just went from there,' I said. 'I wasn't going to let them get away with that.'

Mum's smile faded. 'Elliot, sometimes . . . sometimes people do the wrong thing but for the right reason.'

'I'm not with you,' I said.

'Well, for example, for a while slavery was actually legal. So if ordinary people hadn't fought against a bad law, then it would never have been changed. And in the Second World War, the Nazis passed laws making their discrimination against Jews legal. That was a bad law, too.'

'What has all that got to do with you and me?' I asked.

'Elliot, your uncle and I *did* try to break into the Shelby building. We weren't going to steal anything. We just wanted to make a film of all the rare animals they'd smuggled into their laboratories. Some of those animals are on the endangered species list but at Shelby's they were quite happy to use them in their experiments. Your uncle needed my help – but that doesn't mean that I don't take full responsibility for my own actions.'

I stared at Mum, unable to believe my ears. 'But you told me that the tape was a fake . . .'

'It *was* a fake. Your uncle and I had masks on the entire time. The video tape was doctored.'

'But . . . but . . .'

'I decided you should know the truth,' Mum sighed. 'I've had enough of games and lies.'

I turned to face her. 'Promise me you won't do that any more. Promise me.'

Mum smiled at me. 'I promise. My industrial espionage days are over. I was going to get out anyway, before all this blew up in my face.'

I regarded Mum. It was as if I was seeing her for the very first time. My mum had tried to break into the Shelby building . . .

'Suppose they'd caught you – and I don't just mean on tape?' I asked.

I couldn't help it. I was angry.

'It was a risk we felt we had to take. If no-one stands up to the Shelbys and Pardelas of this world, then they'll soon end up ruling it,' Mum said.

'But you're not going to do it any more?' I insisted.

'No. I think I'll become a freelance secretary. How would that suit you?'

'I'd like that very much.' I replied. And it was the truth!

THE END

About the Author

Born in London in 1962, MALORIE BLACKMAN studied computer science and worked at a variety of different jobs before becoming a full time writer. Although she has travelled throughout Europe and the United States working as a database manager, her ideal position would be captaining the Starship Enterprise – being a real Star Trek fan – or accompanying agent Mulder on one of his action-packed X-Files.

Malorie has had phenomenal success with her first book for Transworld, *HACKER*, which won two major children's awards in 1994: The WH Smith Mind Boggling Books Award, and the Young Telegraph/Gimme 5 Award. She has written a number of other books for children including *OPERATION GADGETMAN!* and *THIEF!* which has been televised for Book Box for Channel 4 Schools and won the 1996 Young Telegraph/Fully Booked Award. Her latest action-packed addition to the Transworld list, *PIG-HEART BOY,* was also shortlisted for several awards.

When she's not working Malorie enjoys messing about on the guitar, piano and saxophone. She goes regularly to the cinema and theatre, enjoys watching TV, playing computer games and surfing the world-wide web. She loves reading absolutely everything – except Westerns!

She lives with her partner in South London with a variety of animals . . . a rabbit, a frog, a leopard, several bears and monkeys, a haggis, a whale – all stuffed toys of course! The latest addition to her collection is her gorgeous little daughter Elizabeth, with whom all the toys get along splendidly.

THIEF!

by Malorie Blackman

Lydia's last thought before darkness closed over her mind was that the strange, swirling storm had trapped her. Would it ever let her go?

It begins with a challenge – to take a school cup and keep it overnight. But when twelve-year-old Lydia is accused of theft – and worse – she can see no way out of the chaos and unhappiness that begins to overwhelm her and her family. No way out but to run away . . .

Fleeing to the bleak, empty moors, a strange, swirling storm suddenly whirls Lydia into the future – where bitterness, pain and hatred have distorted the lives of everyone. Who is the Tyrant who now rules the town? Why has Lydia been brought there? And can she ever get back to her own time? Lydia struggles to find answers. But first, she must endure a terrible confrontation . . .

'Spellbinding . . . must surely establish Malorie Blackman as one of today's oustandingly imaginative and convincing writers' *The Junior Bookshelf*

WINNER OF THE YOUNG TELEGRAPH/FULLY BOOKED AWARD

0 552 52808 0